"And these the Devil's marks be insensible
and being pricked will not bleed
and be often in their secretest parts
and therefore require diligent and careful search."

-Michael Dalton,* The Countrey Justice, *1618

The Mark
Arla Dahl

ISBN-13: 978-0-9904016-3-6

Published by Brooklyn Rose Press

www.arladahl.com

Cover & Design by Kolleen Shallcross

TESTIMONIALS

...a breathtaking tale of accusation and innocence, dominance and submission, fear and lust, set amid the charged atmosphere of seventeenth-century witch hysteria. I defy you not to squirm and moan right along with Abigail as you read The Mark."

- best-selling author Pam McKenna

"An exceptionally erotic trip into the past..."

- award-winning author Bianca D'Arc

"This original and thought-provoking piece of erotic fiction is beautifully written and captivating. It kept me on the edge of my seat and completely spellbound."

- Chloe and Sabine's Smart Mouth Smut

"At times, I felt like covering my eyes, and yet, I couldn't keep from peeking through my fingers!"

-author, Pamela Hearon

ACKNOWLEDGMENTS

It isn't until the pressure is on when one fully realizes how much they depend on the support of friends and family. I am extremely fortunate to have had that support from the people around me, and my deepest thanks go out to them:

My ultra-talented and generous friend and designer, Kolleen Shallcross who saw my vision for this book, cleaned it up and created something so much better.

For Gwendolyn Petrarch and Lisa Shulman, who cared not how many revisions I made but would read again and again.

For Linda Ford, who has been my sounding board and calming presence, always guiding me forward while holding the paddle lest I dare throw up my hands and claim defeat.

For Amy, Lynne, LisaJo, Sharon, Patty and Pam. Thank you for reading the scratch copies of this and for cheering me on.

And of course, to my family for allowing me to bombard them with what-if scenarios about scenes they probably did not want to visualize.

I could not have completed this project without all of you.

Immoral Virtue Trilogy

by *Arla* Dahl

Book One

The Mark

"All witchcraft comes from carnal lust,
which is in women insatiable."

~Heinrich Kramer, 1486
"Malleus Maleficarum" (*The Hammer of Witches*)

DEDICATION

To the innocent victims of that cruel dark time when evil danced in the hearts of the accusers and not in the souls of the accused.

FROM THE AUTHOR

Dear Reader,

In 1692, it was understood that a witch's body bore the mark of the beast. It could be nearly any type of mark. It could appear and disappear. It could show itself as black, or blue...

However it looked, whenever it appeared, the mark would most often be in some hidden spot, and it would be insensitive to even the deepest prick of a pin. Those accused of witchcraft – most often women rather than men – would be publicly stripped then intimately searched and tested for this mark.

What if... instead of searching for places on their flesh that were deadened to pain, the examiner searched for places that could be awakened by pleasure?

So it is in my wicked little village, Wedick Colony, where the accused must choose whether to submit to the governor's private examination, or to resist and be subjected to a very public examination by the villagers. It is not much of a choice, but at least here, unlike in history, it is their choice to make. And once made, they will be forced to feel pleasure, to have their sighs heard and proved true. Only then will they be declared unmarked for it is known that only a witch cannot feel. But should they resist, fail to cry out, whether in pain or in pleasure, then all will know they have been marked by the beast.

I hope you enjoy this twist of history. And I hope you find pleasure within these pages.

May you be unmarked.

Arla

The Mark

Arla Dahl

"Their sayd familiars
hath some big or little teat
borne by the witch upon their body,
and in some secret place,
where he sucketh there."
- *Michael Dalton, 1618*

Wedick Colony, 1682 - At the Midnight Moonrise

The forest exhaled a pungent odor only sunlight could subdue, but sunlight would not grace the wicked until this deed had been done. The six women, having been bound to the great oak's gnarled and aged limbs for six hours and six minutes, shivered from fear and frigid weather. They yearned for daylight as much as they dreaded its coming. Whimpering, they were led from the forest through town, wrists secured one to the other.

Night fought daybreak as the devil would fight a prayer. Cold flowing mists rose waist-high, and woodland creatures stirred and scurried. Torch-bearing townsfolk gathered despite it all, watching as the women were brought into the governor's massive gated lair.

"Witches will get theirs," someone hissed.

"Burn them," said another.

"Bare them for us all! Let us see what they hide!"

The crowd grew louder. Demanding the women be exposed, the devil's marks be located. Beyond the din, the accused kept eyes downcast lest they be flogged as well as bared.

The manor doors opened and a hush fell upon the crowd. Governor Jameson Foster's towering silhouette filled the doorway, stance wide, arms akimbo. "Prepare them!"

A cheer followed his bellowed order. The crowd inched closer. The accused were bound again, wrists and ankles, to massive wooden X's anchored in the ground. The watchman – his face covered by a black hood so the beast could not see him, come after him, condemn him – stood before the last woman he tied. He snatched the neck of her frayed shift in his meaty hands and ripped it to the waist.

Her cries were drowned by the cheering crowd as her breasts were bared for all to see.

The next shift was torn, breasts bared, nipples hard from the icy air. The next as well. And on down the line, until all the women, their faces ablaze with the heat of humiliation, were naked to the waist.

They had chosen this. Had hoped it would free their souls from Satan's hold. Hoped by releasing pride, submitting to inspections, their names would be cleared. Their lives spared.

The crowd drew closer. Staring. Ogling. Laughing. Both fearful and joyous that the devil's marks might be found.

And then their beloved governor strode down the stairs, a lazy gait that showed his bravery, his command over the accused and their demon. He reached the first woman. Abigail, no more than twenty.

Her blue eyes, wide and red-rimmed, beseeched him to make quick work of this indignity, then set her free. He would not. He could not. Every one of the women would be fully inspected – by his eyes, his hands, his fingers – until he was satisfied they were not stained, anywhere, by The Mark. Or until he was satisfied they were.

He stared down into her eyes. Unsure if in their depths he saw truth or lies. And then his gaze dipped lower, caressed her breasts as they hung before him, heaving from her shallow yet rapid breaths. Her flesh was white as mother's milk. Her nipples taut and pink. They begged for his inspection.

Ever so slowly, he raised a hand, lightly took her right nipple between thumb and forefinger then squeezed, relishing the sound of her sharp gasp. If she could feel his touch, then her nipples were pure, not tainted by the devil – for spots marred by him were dead even to the deepest prick of a pin.

He pinched harder, enough to hold fast as he lifted her breast to inspect the flesh below. White, pure. Lovely. Without releasing her, or gentling his hold, he did the same to the other breast, pinching hard, squeezing until the satisfying moan came from her frightened mouth.

Her lips quivered and he longed to encourage her. But if he touched his mouth to hers in comfort and the devil were inside her, the devil would enter him as well. Better to inspect her every part before providing the comfort innocence inevitably welcomed.

He let go, watched her breasts drop into place, then turned away and beckoned the watchman. "Cut her loose."

Her eyes darted from the watchman's work as he untied her, to the crowd and back.

Jameson could assure her, tell her he meant only to strip her binds and escort her inside, away from prying eyes, where he would inspect her fully. But fear and uncertainty loosened the devil's grip, and he would be a fool to distract her from that.

Her arms were freed first, then her legs, yet she remained, spread, looking at him, as if seeking permission to move. With patience a virtue, he tested hers. Held her gaze with his, then let it drift slowly over her bare breasts, her spread legs. A woman so eager to expose herself this way would only be an innocent. Or so it had been in the past.

Never had one who willingly submitted showed a trace of The Mark on her body. Those who fought the probe were exposed as witches. And punished. They had a wildness in their eyes. A dark panic unlike that of the innocent. A daring, mocking look that drew anger from him. Surely, that, too, was the devil's work, since anger was not normally Jameson's to feel.

With a flick of his hand, he gave his permission, and she lowered her arms to her sides. The torn gaping shift covered one breast. He reached out, touched a finger to the edge of the fabric at her shoulder, brushed it downward, over the chilled surface of her flesh. His fingertip reached her nipple and he pressed, rubbed hard circles over it. First in one direction, then the other. She shuddered and he smiled, sure from her genuine responses that she was indeed an innocent.

Tradition dictated the next few minutes, and he pushed the shift aside, uncovering her breasts fully, then turned her toward the crowd.

Standing behind her, he grabbed the fabric at her shoulders and drew it down to her elbows.

The crowd let out a cheer. They, too, must have noticed how her neck and arms were free of The Mark.

In one fist, he held the gathered fabric behind her, forcing her arms back, her chest out, and steered her toward the crowd so they might clearly see her purity. They reached for her and she stumbled backward, against him.

"Be brave, little one," he said softly. "It is their right, and your life." With the fabric still in his fist, he shoved her toward the outstretched hands. "Be this a witch?"

The crowd, old and young men, women of the same ages, touched her, inspected her breasts as he had done. Pinching, lifting. Leaning in closer to see her purity for themselves. Several squeezed her flesh in their palms, then cheered again when she cried out.

He walked her down the line, let everyone have their fill, then pulled her out of reach. "Enough!"

The girl shivered. Yet another sign of innocence. She felt the cold and the shame. She had chosen wisely. Her submission to his inspection spared her the indignity of being brutally and thoroughly examined by the eager crowd. He would make quick work of it, then get to the others before day broke. He glanced at the sky. Though sunlight was still hours away, six required inspection this night. It was more than ever before.

He turned to the watchman. "You!" Pointed to the women still bound. "Begin as I did." Then pointed to the crowd. "Satisfy these good people, then shackle the accused until my return."

Setting his back on the rowdy crowd, he brought Abigail toward the manor, guiding her to his rooms and shutting the door behind them.

His fist still at her back, he brought her to the center of his antechamber. Though she did not resist, she trembled so violently that he felt the vibration to his shoulder. He released her slowly, prepared to catch her should she fall to the floor in fear. To his delight, she remained upright, shoulders held back. She would cooperate and he would soon reward her.

He left her there where she might feel heat from the hearth, and lit candles around the room. He placed one on the stand before a mirror on the wall, set more on the mantle and some on the wide wooden table. He placed another beside the chest that held all he needed to examine her.

Kneeling before the chest, he turned the key. The lock gave way with a harsh metal sound that sliced through the silent room. She gasped and he spared a glance at her rigid back.

"Hush," he said, noting her awareness, her terror.

He would not yet encourage her for he knew, from many past, the coming moments would not be easy. No part of her would remain unseen or untested. The witch would have some hidden place deadened to pain, no matter how skillfully prodded. The innocent would feel it all.

The hinges creaked as he raised the lid and rested it back against the wall. The sound hovered in the air around them like a death bell's hollow tolling. He took a small crop from his supply within the chest and crossed the room to stand in front of her.

Warm muted light bathed her body. The heated air softened and smoothed her nipples. Her breathing had calmed and her gaze was lowered as if she slept while standing.

"You will not look away from me, Abigail."

She lifted her wide eyes to his.

He reached for a candle on the mantle, held it between them for a better view of her face, noted no sign of deception. "Do you understand?"

"I do."

If he were a breath further from her, he would not have heard her whispered reply.

He set the candle back, then adjusted it to reflect from the mirror above the mantle. He shifted another candle to create more light. "Why are you here, Abigail?"

"I am here to prove my innocence."

Slowly, he turned back to her. "Then you freely choose your fate this hour?"

She lowered her eyes and seemed to shudder. As he drew a breath to admonish her for averting her gaze, she looked at him and hesitantly replied. "Aye, Good Sir, I do."

He watched her a moment before turning away. The willing were always willing until the inspection progressed. Though willing or not, the deed would be done.

He went to the wide table and sat back against its edge. "Then we are to begin," he said and settled the crop across his thighs. "Disrobe."

Oh, the indignity of baring herself to him in this perfunctory way when wrapped in his arms had been her secret wish these last two years.

"Did you not hear me well?"

She had heard him and willed herself to obey but the way he looked at her, as if he saw her as a woman not a witch, made her hesitate. Eager to show him all she had, reluctant to do so as one of the accused.

A slow blink was her only reprieve from looking into his dark eyes. She blinked again. Then she reached for the cuff at her wrist, pulled the drawstring there and eased an arm free. His gaze left her face to travel her body, and her movements became stilted and shaky.

When both arms were free, she stood naked from the waist up, and the torn shift lay draped over her petticoat. It was all that hid him from her most private parts, since the accused were allowed only a light shift, petticoat and soft slippers. Nothing more. Her fingers lingered on the bow at her waist. She wanted to end this but could not bring herself to do so.

His fist tightened on the crop in his lap and she feared the sting of it should she not comply. As she made to open the bow, she noticed the depth of his breathing. There was more to his attention than inspection, of that she was sure, but such knowledge did not comfort. Mayhap he would see her distress and allow her to close her eyes so she might imagine this baring as less shameful.

He stood abruptly. "Do not dawdle."

She stumbled backward. "Forgive me." She did not mean to resist. She knew the consequence of such an act – submit to him by choice or to the villagers by force.

"You said you understood…"

Tears sprung to her eyes. "I do, Good Sir, pray forgive me." This shame was hard enough. How would she bear it if he tossed her to the crowd?

"You are not the only one this night." He had softened his voice though his tone remained stern. "You will not waste precious time."

"Nay, I will not." She locked her gaze on his as he had ordered and broke it only to blink tears from her eyes.

He touched a warm finger to her cheek and wiped her tears as they fell. "You might save these for later." His fingertip lingered at her jaw a moment before he dropped his hand to his side. "Clasp your hands behind you."

She did without thought or hesitation. She kept her eyes on his as he looked from her face to her breasts now thrust out toward him. Though she tried to reign in her breathing, it came in short, shuddering bursts, but he seemed not to care.

He raised the crop and touched the cool, stiff leather tip to her throat. "My intent is not to hurt you, Abigail." He dragged the crop down, haltingly, between her breasts. "But it is only a witch who does not feel." Her belly quivered as he drew the crop lower still, not stopping until it reached the bow at her waist. He let it linger there, no longer cool against her flesh, then drew it back up at the same lazy pace, as if her flesh were a canvas he painted. "Do you understand?"

She tried to speak but had no voice and nodded instead.

He smoothed the crop back down and traced the under curve of her left breast, his gaze closely following the path of it. "Lift your chin."

The instant she did, she felt the icy sting of the crop against her breast. She cried out, more in shock than in pain. She made to block the second blow to the same spot, but remembered herself, and clasped her hands behind her again. The leather smoothed over the now tender spot and she braced herself as the third sting came.

"Be happy for the pain," he said calmly, "to not feel it would mean you have been stained."

He tapped the crop several times to the side of her breast, bouncing it lightly, as if judging the movement. She fought to hold back the sob of humiliation and pain. No, not pain. An incredible ache. A sharp pang she could wipe away if permitted to do so. But this light tapping and his eyes intent on her breast, made her yet more aware of the sensation there.

He drew his hand back and lifted his eyes to hers, then, with a flick of his wrist, struck the crop against the top of her breast, each side, and below.

Each strike made her gasp, made her breast bob. And then in rapid succession he struck her nipple. Twice. Three times. Five. Six. The sound of it slapping filled her ears.

She lost count as he continued to punish that tiny bit of her. All she was - heart, mind, soul - centered on that one part of her body, she felt nothing else, thought of nothing else. The sting of each strike coursed through her, from her nipple down to her belly and lower, creating an ache, a sudden throbbing below her petticoat. She pressed her thighs together, tried to soothe the budding sensations, but felt no relief. Only heat and a wet pulsing need.

This should not happen - to be aroused by this examination. If a witch could not feel pain, could she feel pleasure? She blinked at tears, barely kept from covering her sore breast with one hand and burying the other between her legs.

Finally, the strikes ended and the only sounds in the room were her heavy panting and slight whimpers. He studied her eyes, her face, and when he lowered his gaze, she all but felt the heat of it against her now sensitive flesh.

He switched the crop to his other hand and she nearly cried out, ready to beg him to spare her. Only fear of being sent to the crowd stopped her from speaking - fear and a desire for him to continue, to finish this and clear her name.

He struck her other breast as he did the first - several taps on all sides, a light bouncing on which he focused full attention.

She felt herself clench, anticipating the strikes to her nipple. Counted them. Counted the beat between strikes, too. Found the rhythm and breathed with it, inhaling between blows, exhaling gruffly when contact was made.

With each slap, with each breath, she felt a tightening in her core, so strong, so hot, she worried he would notice, and tried to will the sensations away.

The hot stinging stopped, yet her breasts tingled as if it continued.

On a gasp, she opened her eyes. Realizing too late she had closed them, had let her head lag back and breathed heavily through her now dry mouth. How wanton she must have seemed.

His gaze roamed over her in a slow but steady caress, showing no awareness of the growing wetness between her legs or the ache that had yet to subside.

He tucked the crop's stout handle into a leather pouch at his hip. "Turn around," he said softly, returning his gaze to hers. "Lift your hair from your neck."

She did as he instructed, feeling even more vulnerable with her arms above her head and her hair cascading through her fingers than she had with her arms clasped at her back.

She caught her reflection in a mirror across the room and for a moment was unsure if it was herself looking back. Her pale face was flushed as she had never seen, not even in the coldest of winters. Her dry lips were red as if she had been kissed long and hard.

She ran her tongue over them to moisten, then looked into her own eyes - no more tears and no defiance. Just what was required and expected. Acceptance. She almost smiled. She had felt every blow and withstood them all. She could endure the rest. No matter what came next.

She lifted her chin without being told, but her bravery faltered as he came to stand behind her. He captured her gaze through the mirror, then dropped it to her breasts. Her own gaze fell, and, with a gasp, she noted the angry red marks he had left there.

He cupped her breasts in his large, warm hands. Kneaded them lightly, as she would have done to soothe the ache. But his hands, handling her so gently now after beating her so, did not soothe. They stirred and shamed. Her eyes fluttered shut a second before she remembered to keep them on his. He was looking back at her through the mirror, watching, gauging her responses. Under his scrutiny her face grew hot and her breathing faltered.

He leaned in closer and his warm deep breaths tickled her neck, her shoulder. It rippled along her naked flesh. Gently, he rolled her sore nipples between his fingers. She winced, both in pain and in pleasure as the tingling heat between her legs grew more intense. She struggled to subdue it, wished for an end to his touches before they consumed her.

"You find this difficult."

She fought to find her voice. "Most difficult."

He nodded slowly, kept his eyes on hers through the mirror, his fingers still fondling her. And then he let go and stood back just a breath.

He raised a hand and she tried to steel herself, unsure which to fear more, his touch or the crop. When his fingertips brushed down the length of her spine, she could not suppress the shuddering breath or rippling warmth that surged like a wave straight down to her core.

He brushed them back up then swept the fingertips of both hands down her neck, searing paths to her shoulders, along her arms and up to her hands in her hair. She had trusted inner strength to get her through this, but his every touch weakened her. He awakened her flesh, made her feel both ashamed of her raw nakedness and ignited by it. Her breasts felt even fuller, heavier, and she wanted nothing more than to drop her hands from her hair and cup them herself, both to cover and to caress.

With his head tipped just enough so she could not see his eyes, he stood to one side. She lowered her own eyes enough to watch his fingers skim the flesh at her rib. She drew a ragged breath as he smoothed them just above the band at her waist, from one side, along her back, then to the other, tickling her, making her tense as he stepped slowly around her. He repeated the move, his fingers traveling slightly higher, tracing lazily over her back, her sides, then starting again. Her flesh felt scorched by these gentle touches, then cooled by their absence.

When he reached the middle of her back she thought she could take no more. No man had ever touched her this way. No one warned that he would. None of the accused before her said how he had behaved, or what had occurred, only that the sole devil in the room had been the governor himself. Only now could she guess their meaning.

Though she had hoped this would be quick, a look at her most private parts and then a dismissal, she knew now it would go on until he drove her mad with need. Was she to submit to that as well? He was to learn what she felt since only a witch would feel nothing. Was it this feeling, too, that he wanted to test?

"The mark." His softly spoken words drew her from her thoughts before the shocked tone of his voice fully reached her. "You bear the mark."

Understanding slammed through her and her gaze flew to his through the mirror. And then she saw it, on her right breast. The black mark of the beast.

Terror threatened to freeze her in place. She fought against it, wrenched herself from his hold as he snatched at her arms.

"No!" She ran to the mirror. "It is but a smudge on the glass!" She scrubbed her palm over the spot, turned at his approach. "I am innocent! Look again…" She cupped her breasts in her hands, lifted them in offering. "I am not stained."

He froze mid-step, staring at her unblemished flesh as if he had difficulty believing his own eyes.

Taking courage from that reprieve, she let her breasts fall and pulled at the bow on her petticoat, letting it slide down her legs and pool at her feet, taking her torn shift with it until she stood naked before him. "I am innocent. You will see." Her voice trembled as much as her body, but she did not care. She would do what had to be done for him to see her directly and not through the looking glass. "I am innocent."

He grabbed the hair at the back of her head, bringing his body against hers. His quilted linen doublet brushed her nipples as she breathed hard against him, sending hot sparks of fear through her.

"You are a witch." Anger and disbelief colored his tone.

She tried to shake her head, but his hold on her hair was too tight. "It was but a smudge." She would make him forget what he saw. Whatever it took, however long. She would cooperate fully, endure his crop, his hands - whatever he required - and she would convince him he was wrong. She wedged her hands between their bodies, forced him back just an inch.

"Look at me," she said on a breath, and smoothed her hands into the soft curls between her legs. "I beg you."

He let go of her and stood back, his angry gaze slowly dropping.

She tipped her hips forward. "I feel everything," she said then lightly pinched her nether lips and peeled herself open for him. "Test me as you please, and you will see."

Chapter Three

He could look only at her sex as it dripped with deceit. He yanked the crop from the pouch on his hip, raised it and aimed.

Her terrified sob cut through his fury, stopping him mid-swing. Her tear-filled eyes locked on his, pleading. But for what? Mercy? Or the punishment she knew she deserved?

She had purposely hidden the truth, betrayed his benevolence, while he thought only to comfort and calm. A witch so bold would not flinch, no matter how harsh her punishment might be, though his wish was for her to feel every strike.

He tightened his fist on the handle, took a step closer and smelled the heady scent of her fear, her lust. Her muffled whimpers rocked her body as she stood there, spread, trembling. Blemish-free. Only the few welts from his exam marred her body, changing the exquisite beauty of her full breasts from innocent to well-used.

The sight of her licked at something deep inside of him, made him swell in response. He tried to will away the feeling, but failed as his urge to punish her warred with something else. Something unfamiliar. The desire to soothe her, hold her. Have her. It should not be, this ache, this driving need.

He went to the hearth, slapped the crop to the mantle and pressed his palm to it, wanting as much to crush the vile tool as grab it again and use it against her – both for her display of the mark as for her affect on him.

Her harsh panicked breaths were loud in the silent room, adding weight to his confusion. Would she fear what she could not feel? Would she offer herself if she could?

He gave a quick glance toward the mirror, noted the smeared imprint of her palm. He had all but condemned her before testing the spot, before seeing it with his own eyes, not through the glass. Perhaps she was not so bold as brave.

Locking his gaze on hers again, he considered the evidence further. She withstood the exam so far, showed fear and sensitivity to the crop and to his hands. Now, spread and glistening before him, there lingered no sign of the mark, nor had it been there before.

And what of her effect on him? Surely, a witch could not arouse him so. No. He had forgotten himself. She was the accused, he the examiner. His body's response was his failing, not the work of the beast.

He gave her a tight nod. "It was but a smudge."

She released a sob he felt in his own chest, then dropped to her knees and buried her face in her hands.

He permitted her the moment, watched her closely as she cried, naked and folded on the floor. Each ragged breath jostled her breasts, the same as when they had been struck by the crop. Her responses had baited him, challenged him to strike harder, and with each flick of his wrist, she had cried out, moaned, filled the space between them with the scent of her arousal. A scent that hovered still.

Engorged past pain, he took an awkward step toward her, then stopped and cursed need for its persistence. He dared not move as a torturous, cock-twitching wave of pleasure and pain all but emptied him. He breathed through it, fought for at least one mere scrap of control.

He turned away from the sight of her, forced himself to focus on the tasks ahead. He set a kettle of water to heat on the hearth. Without a glance her way, he strode to the table and moved the candles he had set there to a ledge on the wall above it. Better to prepare the table now, while she did not watch, than to have her grow fearful and resistant as understanding dawned.

He took a handful of leather strips from a pile on the ledge and chose four according to length. He looped each through iron rings mounted at the table's four corners, then, with eyes closed, sat back against the table's wide edge and breathed fully.

Slowly, finally in full control, he looked at her and saw only an accused. "Abigail."

With a gasp, she scrambled to her feet. Sniffed back tears and awkwardly tried to block her breasts and her sex from view with her arms, her hands.

He waited for her to settle and when she did not, he folded his arms across his chest and tipped his head in challenge. “Only those with the mark hide what they have.”

It seemed a struggle for her to lower her arms and clasp her hands behind her. Finally she did. A brief moment later, she drew a long breath and lifted her chin.

Though tempted to commend her composure, he refrained. “Take the crop from the mantel and bring it here.”

Her soft slippers swept the floor as she inched toward the mantel and grabbed the crop. His gaze scanned her lovely body as she moved toward him, her breasts and hips swaying with each step. Her hand trembled as she held the crop out to him. When he was through with this examination, he would lay her beneath him and make her whole body tremble. He would forget the women who waited, the townsfolk and all, and see that her every inch was covered in his scent, his seed, for surely a joining with her would wring him dry.

He set his hands in his lap lest she see her affect on him, then inclined his head toward a spot on the table. “Lay it there.”

Her hair brushed his shoulder as she set the crop beside him. A slight curl lingered there as she turned and lifted her gaze to his. He fondled the strand, marveled at its silken texture then arranged it in front of her shoulder just so, grazing his fingertips down to the end where it reached her breast. His gaze traveled the path of his fingertips – over the tops of each breast and down the valley between them.

Her nipples hardened as his gaze and fingertips touched on them. He pressed a thumb to one, casually rubbed it until it hardened further, watching her eyes as he did so. They fluttered closed in immediate response.

He dropped his hand from her and her eyes slowly opened, then widened as if surprised by her own responses. His smile formed on its own. He tamped it down, pleased at her desire to obey, warmed by her inability to do so.

"Go to the chest," he said, and pointed to it. "You will see two amber vials. Bring them here."

When she turned, he received his first rearview of her. He weighed the sight, imagined the soft white flesh of her rump filling his hands, though not quite spilling from them the way her breasts had. He would mold them, knead them, test them for sensitivity. He would spread them wide and examine the tight bud hidden between them.

Both loving and hating her effect on him, he grasped his arousal through his breeches, squeezing tight as if to deflate it merely by strength of hand.

She knelt daintily and leaned into the chest, offering a new view of herself with splendid abandon. He squeezed himself harder. Breathed deeply until the pain subsided and only a sweet throbbing ache remained.

He palmed the crop, then laid it in his lap when she turned back to him.

"Set them here," he said pointing to where the crop had just been. "Then lean forward, flatten yourself to the wood and grasp the far end of the table."

She hesitated only a moment, then bent over and stretched to reach the other side, her fingertips barely touching.

He stood behind her, admired the plumpness of her buttocks, noted a small mole on her left cheek where it met her thigh. He pinched it, smiled as she gasped and quivered. He tapped the crop to the spot. Once. Twice. A third time harder. Waited for the spot to redden, to prove it was not dead.

When it did, he turned his attention to the rest of her rounded flesh. Cupped a palm to one cheek, and squeezed, then smoothed his hand over every inch, testing for any abnormality, feeling only silken skin. He cupped the other cheek, squeezed hard and tipped his head for a closer look at the impressions left by his fingers, first turning her flesh colorless then red. He smacked it lightly, watched it jiggle in response. Then, he started at the small dimple where her back met her rump and skimmed his hand down, his thumb slipping between her cheeks, grazing over her anus, getting her ready for what was to come.

Her only response was a shift in her breathing and though it pained him to think he must hurt her, he had no choice.

"Push up onto your toes," he said. "So you might secure a better hold on the table."

She did as instructed, adjusting herself until her calf muscles strained and her rump was raised higher.

He smoothed the crop along her outer thigh, slowly, a small reminder to her of leather against flesh. A whimper of protest came from her.

"Hush now," he said, though he understood. "You should not fear this." The more intense the exam, the more reluctant the accused were to submit. "You felt it before."

He brushed the crop up to her hip then slowly across one cheek. "If you are unmarked, it will be the same." He lifted the crop from her body, then dabbed it to a new spot on the same smooth cheek.

She gasped, clenched.

He repeated the move - lifting the crop from her then lightly touching it to random spots on her lovely white rump.

"And you willing bear the pain." It was not a clear question, but he expected an answer, for many were the accused who withdrew consent. "I will hear the words."

"I…"

He slid the crop between her cheeks, poked lightly then withdrew it. Pleased to hear her gasp and see her flinch as she acknowledged the feeling. "You…?" He drew his arm back.

"…willingly bear it."

The sharp whack of the crop against the fleshiest part of her mingled with her startled cry. He gave her a second to catch her breath, to get accustomed to the sensation, then swished his arm from the elbow - striking her left and right, up and down. Varying the pace, letting the leather tip land unexpectedly, creating a crisscrossing pattern of red, though using only minimal strength, not wishing to harm her, just awaken her senses.

She cried out as each lash hit its mark, but her cries were no more or less than when he had tested her breasts.

"Stand wide," he said and used his foot to nudge her slippered feet apart. "Hold tighter, do not let go."

He released a volley of strikes where her rump met her thighs. Listened for her breathy responses, watched the flesh redden, careful not to strike the same spot too often. Whack after whack of leather against flesh filled his ears, mingled with her moans until the now-familiar scent of her arousal filled his senses.

Breathless as she, he set the crop on the table. He cupped his palms to her blazing hot flesh. Her body jerked in response and he allowed himself a small smile, relieved as he was by her responses. Her cheeks filled his hands as he had imagined, they were pliant and soft, and conformed to the shape of his palms as he squeezed them, pressed them together then pulled them apart. He spread them wider, examined her tight bud with his eyes, realized she would need more time and attention before he inspected her there.

"You may flatten your feet to the floor now," he said, "but remain bent over as you are."

She relaxed her legs and he continued his ministering, massaging her, hoping to soothe the pain he had inflicted. The way she clenched and quivered, told him he was making it worse.

He let go of her, needing to put space between them as much for her comfort as for his control. He lifted the smaller of the two vials she had brought from the chest. Pulled the stopper and poured a few drops of its sharp woodsy oil into his palm.

"You have done well," he said as he rubbed the rosemary oil into the new welts he had created. "I am pleased."

He dripped more oil into his palms, smoothed it slowly over every sore heated inch of her. "This will soothe the ache," he said then lifted the bottle again and dripped oil into the deep crevasse between her cheeks, massaging them, making sure the oil penetrated her flesh.

"You… wish to soothe me?"

The breathless tone of her voice confirmed what he already knew from her scent. She was still as aroused as he. No witch could find pleasure in this for she could not feel. He swelled even more at the thought of testing her further, of proving her worth and granting her release.

"I wish to test," he said, in answer to her question. "Not torture." He pulled the stopper from the larger vial and poured a few drops of its heavy unscented oil onto the table. "Though I fear you will mistake each as the same."

He scooped up some of the thick oil with his pinky, coating it fully.

She clenched her eyes as if blocking all vision would block all feeling, for his every touch was torture. But it was not to be, for in her mind she saw his gaze fixed and intense as he studied her rump, raised and jutted for his inspection.

She had witnessed crazed ruttings in the woods, had made to turn away. The shame of such a vision had heated her face, her limbs, her core. But she could not move for the sight and the sounds compelled her to watch, to touch herself, to probe her wet aching passage with her fingers until her body shuddered as if in a fit.

Even as her maiden blood tinged her fingers and fear washed over her tingling body, cries of both pain and bliss came from the woman. And the man, pounded away at her, his back arched, his growl primal. She never imagined herself positioned the same as the woman had been, bent over, rump high in offering. And certainly never as an accused witch.

But the pleasure… it was not hers for shame overpowered. She gripped the table until her fingertips hurt. Anything to distract her from thoughts of him behind her, striking her, looking, touching.

His hands skimming her flesh, were hot. Rough and gentle at the same time. Purposefully squeezing her, painfully at times, yet somehow filling her with a hollow aching need she should not feel. She tipped her head lower until her forehead touched the table, unable to bear the humiliation of her own thoughts.

And then the warm rosemary oil he poured and spread onto her rump slid deeply between her fleshy cheeks, tickling her, making that part of her feel slick, alive and tingling. She dipped her hips to let it run off of her, but it clung. She clenched the cheeks of her rump to wipe it away, to rid herself of the sensations there for that was not a spot of which she should be so aware.

She shifted, uncomfortable with this oil so intimately coating her. And then she felt his breath against her, as if he tipped his head closer to see more of her, and breathed deeply upon her flesh.

His hands, his gaze, were on her too close. Too long. She knew not what he sought, and then his fingers spread her cheeks wide even as she fought to hold them tight. All thoughts jumbled in her mind as those fingers easily overpowered, displaying that tiny rear hole until cool air caressed it. He was looking closer still, she felt him lean into her, his clothing brushing her naked hip, and she could not hide. Not from his eyes, not from his touch. Not from the feelings he awakened inside of her.

He murmured something but she did not hear the words. She was dizzy from breathing so hard, from confusing inhale and exhale. She could not keep from trembling as his fingers massaged around that tiny back hole.

She thought of the crowd. Of being outside, at their mercy. Would they be so crude as to touch her this way? She thought of the sinful, rutting couple in the woods. Of their cries of pleasure. Their joining. Like the governor's touch, it was something akin to evil and sorcery for surely it should not arouse her so.

His finger moved slowly over her, circling, testing. And her body responded, surely he must know. What more did he want? Should she cry in fear? In pleasure? Should she push her hips back and scream as the couple in the woods?

Her body screamed. Her body ached. With every smooth circle of his fingertip against her, she found it hard to contract her muscles, as if he wove a spell over them, forcing them to soften. She thought to pull away even as need dripped from her womb, scenting the room, proclaiming its wish for more.

֍

He cupped his left palm to the top of her buttocks, his long fingers reaching midway down. Her muscles tensed beneath his hand and though he wished to calm her, this was still not the time.

Using only his thumb and forefinger, he spread her cheeks wide, exposing her tight puckered passage. Her ragged breaths rocked her body and he leaned into her, holding her steady.

"Breathe deeply," he said and rimmed her anus with the tip of his oiled pinky.

Careful to prepare her, he drew slow circles around the target, drawing closer with each rotation, pressing more firmly as well. She was well oiled, as was his finger, though if she did not relax it would not matter. He spread his thumb and forefinger wider hoping to ease her open a small bit. But, clearly, this part of her was rarely if ever touched, and so access would not be easy.

"You must relax." His voice held more urgency than he intended. He wanted only to finish this and walk away before his erection burst through his seams. Still holding her wide, he again dipped his finger into the oil he had dripped onto the table, then brought his pinky back to her tiny hole and pressed gently.

She cried out and he shushed her.

"Push back," he said, hoping she would. "As if to force me away."

The instant she did, the tip of his finger gained access. She gasped, but did not struggle and he held still. Let her body adjust, then bid her push back again. He waited, his pinky just a knuckle's depth inside of her, barely enough to test her responses.

"Abigail."

"I… cannot."

"It is fear, not pain, that makes you resist, for this is more trying on the mind than the body." Unable to bear this much longer, he kept his pinky in place and smacked his free hand to her. Once, twice. Several more times.

Her hips rocked to and fro, her cries were those of humiliation, for he knew this spanking did not hurt. He watched as her flesh turned a deeper shade of red, then repositioned his hand with thumb and forefinger spreading her wide once more. "Breathe deeply or this will be more trying for body than mind."

She drew two full breaths and released each forcefully, remaining tense throughout.

He watched her closely, withdrew his finger fully and waited for the expected reaction. The instant tension left her, he slid his finger back in, full to the hilt. She bucked in response and he let her, feeling her ring of muscles tighten on his finger, as much holding it there as trying to expel it. Proving sensitivity at least as far as his small finger could reach.

"There now…" He pressed his hand down against her, holding her still and pushed his pinky more firmly inside of her. "…it does not hurt so much."

"It does."

He smiled at the anger in her voice, appreciated her level of shame. No one ever spoke of this examination or what it entailed, and that was good, for if the accused were to know in advance, they might refuse and thus be tossed to the crowd.

"Is it not better to be examined this way than be passed from hand to hand?"

She quickly settled, clearly understanding his meaning.

"We have more to do…" He slid his finger out by a knuckle, then eased it back in again. Ever so gently, he flexed and bent it within her, testing her responses - her whimpers, her struggles - preparing her, mind and body, for the more thorough inspection yet to come.

He smacked his free hand to her rump, a distraction to ease her shame, as he withdrew his finger completely. "You may stand."

He went to the hearth, poured heated water from the kettle over his hands, removing all traces of oil and of her, then dried them by heat of the flame. Without a glance her way, he went back to the table, rested against it, breathing deeply until ready to continue.

"Come here," he said, "and bring the vials with you."

She went to him. Her body trembled, her face was pale and her brows furrowed. But her eyes were dry. For that he was happy but did not say.

He took the vials from her, set the larger one down. "Put out your hands," he said then poured a few drops of the fragrant oil into her palms. "Spread it over your breasts and belly." He set the vial beside the other. "Do not leave one spot dry."

Her delicate hands rubbed over her body in quick strokes, leaving glistening paths behind.

He cupped his hands over hers, stopping her movements. "Slowly," he said, "to cover all in one swipe." He guided her hands over her breasts, smoothed them carefully over every bit of them until a light sheen remained. And then he guided them lower, over her belly, her hips, wiping the excess oil over the tops of her thighs before moving her hands behind her again.

"Clasp them," he said and she did.

Spreading his legs wide to make room for her, he crooked a finger, and she inched forward until her hips brushed his inner thighs and her breasts teased his lips.

"The mark through the glass was as vivid as these welts," he said, touching his fingertips to them. "How could my eyes deceive me so?"

"T'was the glass." Her gaze was lowered to his as she stood before him, her face impassive, her voice matter-of-fact.

He suppressed a smile, appreciating the challenge in her eyes and in her voice. "I accept that now but did not at first." He let his fingers linger against her, as much to reassure himself as to enjoy the slick feel of her flesh. "I was pained as much by the mark as by thoughts that you might have deceived me." The oil allowed him to glide his hands smoothly over her breasts, let her nipples slip through his fingers as he pinched them. "No other deception has wounded me so."

He squeezed her breasts in his palms, dug his fingertips in, feeling for something, anything, that should not be. Only her tender plushness filled his hands. "I only tell you this for your comfort…" Touching her took him well beyond duty to pleasure. "…so you understand I do these things to help you, not hurt you." He had to force himself to remove his hands from her body.

"Do these things you do yet prove my innocence?"

He lifted his gaze to hers. Shook his head slowly. "Not yet."

"There is yet more?" Though she did not blink or look away, fear wrapped itself around her every word, her every breath.

"There is."

"Will it…be difficult?"

"Has it been difficult so far?"

She swallowed noisily, blinked long and hard. "Extremely so."

"Then yes." He got to his feet, set his hands on her hips and inched her backward. "It will be difficult."

Her pretty eyebrows bunched together. "For body or for mind?"

He would not share that truth. If he could stop this now, he would. He would take her into his arms and comfort her. He would lay her beneath him there by the hearth. The raspy sound of her heavy breaths would permeate his thoughts, block out all else, as the slickness of their arousals mingled.

"Can you not tell me?" Her voice was barely a whisper.

He blinked, realized he had been looking down at her as she looked up at him – her eyes expectant, her hands clasped behind her, her breasts against his chest. And his hands on her naked hips.

Control must be his for her sake. And for the others who waited, in the cold. With his judgment of each due by daybreak, time was not his to squander on thoughts of her writhing beneath him.

Stiff with need, he inched her back further, wanting her far from reach. It had never been this way with an accused, not until after he had proven their innocence. Perhaps his arousal was fate insisting on her purity.

"I know not what you hide," he said, "but it has entranced me."

"I cannot hide," she said, "for you have seen more of me than I have seen of myself." As she spoke, a wave of deep crimson tinted her face.

He ached to touch a fingertip to it, to feel its heat, to compare it to the heat of her reddened breasts and buttocks. "I have indeed seen much of you," he said, with a slight bow.

Then, recalling how the sweet scent of her arousal had greeted him, not once or twice, but several times as he touched her, struck her, he leaned closer to her and let his words brush her ear. "Touching and testing you has been my pleasure…and my pain." He lowered his voice further, as if sharing a secret even the walls should not hear. "The same as it has been for you."

He strode past her to the chest, retrieved swaths of cloth and a blade. Without granting himself another glance at her body, he went back to the table and set the items carefully on the ledge above it.

"Come," he said, then used his foot to pull a stool from under the table. "Climb up and sit at the very edge." He offered his hand as she stepped onto the stool. She took it, her fingers ice cold though she had stood near the hearth. Her gaze was averted, but he did not mind this one time.

When she was seated on the table's narrow end, he sat on the stool in front of her. He took a delicate foot into his hands and removed her slipper.

"You will not need these," he said then removed the other, and set both on the floor beneath the table.

He warmed her cold feet with his hands, then cupped his palms to the back of her ankles and felt the chill there as well. He slid his hands higher, over her calves, moving slowly to warm her, touching her gently, aware that what came next would be most trying for her mind.

He stood and placed her feet on the stool.

"Lie back," he said, then set his gaze on the light patch of hair nestled between her thighs, gauging how long it would take to remove.

Could he not hear the hard beating of her heart? Could he not see she was a woman who felt his every touch from her smallest toes to the top of her head?

He had aroused her to a most shameful height. And then, to her horror, had whispered awareness of her arousal, an awareness she had not known he possessed, stripping her of even that bit of dignity. To be spoken to so softly, to be told he cared for her comfort, was pained by her deceit, as if she mattered, only to be ordered to lie back, without explanation… without a hint of what was to come…

He should not speak to her at all, should not look at her with such heat in his eyes when she was no more to him than the other five women awaiting his touch. As if he heard her thoughts, he turned away. She shifted, looked at his broad solid back and steady stride as he went to the chest, then quickly averted her gaze, not wanting to see what he might take from there.

She had once imagined herself with him, but now, when he was convinced of her innocence, when she was freed, she could never look into his eyes again. He had seen too much of her, had coaxed too much of a response from her body, despite her attempts to fight it.

Her face burned with shame at the thought. Even wedded and sharing a bed, no man would touch a woman as he had touched her… bending her over, forcing a finger inside of her, invading her in a most shocking way.

Her insides clenched as she thought of it again, of the feel of his hands soothing the ache of the crop. Of the gentle way he rubbed oil into her flesh, of the intensity of pain mixed with pleasure as his thick solid finger probed her, moved within her, withdrew and plunged back in. His wicked touch made the throbbing heat within her grow yet more intense. Made her more aware of how he watched her, listened to her, waited for her responses which went from horrified gasps to decadent sighs.

If he had not ordered her to grip the table, she might have turned on him, shoved him from her and run outside, beseeching the crowd for mercy, for surely they did not know what he did within these walls.

He would have caught her, stopped her mid-flight. And she would have begged him to ease the ache of need he had caused, knowing well how shameful and vulgar that would be.

Even now, sitting naked upon the table and looking at his back as he went from the chest to the hearth, she both sought and dreaded his touch.

A witch could not feel. She had heard so many times. If he knew of these feelings clashing within her, of this sinful lust she felt for him now, would it not prove her pure? Though purity of mind was not hers.

She covered her face with her hands, tried to sort through her thoughts, herself confused as to her own guilt or innocence. She had witnessed relations no pure woman should witness. Had probed her own body, breached her own maidenhead…

With a sudden thought, she raised her head and dropped her hands to her naked lap. Would he see? Would he believe she had taken her own virtue or would he declare it the work of the beast?

The scrape of metal against metal drew her attention back to him as he lifted a kettle from the hearth, his hand protected from the heat by a heavy cloth. Surely he would know. He was young but wise. A man like Jameson Foster, as governor in charge of these examinations, would have seen these breaches before. He would know the truth.

He had told her to lie back. She dared not challenge him. To display such an obstinate spirit would be to suggest dalliance with the devil, to confess without words. No. She would obey no matter how difficult the command. She would convince his mind, if not his eyes, of her innocence. The same as she had done before.

With a shuddering breath, she laid against the cool wood which quickly warmed beneath her. Her heart still beat heavily. Her breaths were erratic. Her feet were cold and pressed to the stool. What would he do to her? Scald her? Stick her? There had been whispers of what some endured at the hands of their examiners. Of witches being burned or poked with pins. Of sensitive flesh being pricked until the pain grew so great it blurred all reason, rendered the accused senseless and caused them to ignore it, not cry out and thus be found guilty. How would she bear that pain if she could not bear the very thought of it?

Had he done this too? No. Not their beloved governor. Though no one spoke of what he had done. Their shame, no doubt, too great.

Tears of her own shame, of confusion and fear, blurred her view of the candelabra as it hung above her. She squeezed her eyes closed, let the tears slip down the sides of her face and into her hair. His boots thudded heavily on the wood floor as he neared her. With great effort, she tried to steady her breath and force her eyes open so she might look at him as he had commanded.

He set the kettle beside her legs on the table. Though she welcomed the heat of it, the heat of his eyes on her body seemed to burn right through her. He dropped the thin handle and it clinked against the kettle. Its harsh sound, his hard look, and her chilled body, naked before him, were all that existed at that moment. She dared not imagine what might come next for no matter what vision she had, she feared his actions would be much worse.

❧

Though he allowed for hesitation, she had taken every second he had been prepared to give before she did as instructed and laid back. When the sound of her shifting against the wood abated, he had turned, and if not for the weight of the water to hold him back, he might have forgotten himself and charged forward to ravish the beauty before him.

He forced each step to slow. Steadied as much his body as his mind, aware that what was to come needed a most stable hand. Once he set the kettle down, he wedged the heavy cloth he had used on the handle between it and her flesh, not wanting to burn her.

She did not move but to breathe heavily, and for that he was pleased, for she, too, must remain steady.

Though he felt the heat of the hearth through to his bones, her flesh was dimpled from cold. Her breasts rose and fell with her rapid breaths, her nipples were stiff. Her arms were down at her sides and her hands in fists. He circled his fingers around one small wrist, then gently brought her arm up over her head.

"The binds will not hurt." He wrapped her wrist with the small leather strap he had looped through the iron ring at the corner, then lifted her other arm and tied it the same on the opposite side. She whimpered but did not resist, and he took pity on her. "It is merely to keep you from harming yourself."

He grabbed the large amber vial, put it beside the kettle so it might warm, then smoothed his palm down her raised arm, over her cool breast, her belly, pausing as he made his way to the foot of the table to examine a dull mark at her hip. He scratched at it with his fingernail, noted how she quivered in response.

"I will position you," he said as he moved past the kettle and cupped his hand to her knee. "You will not struggle. Do you understand?"

Her lips moved, her breaths came quicker, but she did not respond.

He offered some comfort. "This will pass quickly if you obey." He accepted her slight nod as surrender then took her ankles in his hands and lifted her feet from the stool. "Bend your knees," he said, and when she did, he raised her legs until her heels were pressed to the table's edge.

He poured some of the fragrant oil into his hand, warmed it between his palms, then smoothed it over the inside of her left thigh, pushing her leg back and out to the side, stretching her, forcing her leg wider, her ankle closer to the corner where he secured it with the third leather strap. He did the same to her other leg, oiling her inner thigh, stretching her wide, then securing her. He set the small vial on the shelf and stood back to admire how beautifully spread and ready he had made her.

ଔ

Warm need flooded her body with every stroke of his hands on her thighs. She ached to cover herself, to shield her rising ardor from him, yet she could not, for the binds at her wrists and her ankles held her back.

If she were not tied, she would not harm herself. She would plunge her hands between her legs, both of them, in a frenzied rush of movement, touching, rubbing, even probing, seeking relief from the hot pounding need his every touch fashioned within her. She would not care that her fingers further breeched her maidenhead. She would find release.

Surely he knew of this, for everywhere he looked, she ached, she dripped. If she could find her voice she would plead with him to untie her. To set her free. To let her cover herself for she could not bear to be displayed so crudely.

Yet even as her mind protested, her body craved, betraying her in a most haunting and shameful way. His hungry eyes devoured her, and his hands, hot again on her thighs, slowly kneaded them. Her hips twitched, seeking both escape from his touch and more of it.

ⴰ

He would dream of her scent for many a night as it was a potent aroma he could not soon forget. The fragrant juices seeped from her, leaving a glistening path from her tight passage to her anus, and pooling below her on the table. He ached to scoop it up with his fingers, inhale it, taste it. Lap at its source until she screamed with pleasure.

He squeezed the flesh of her thighs tighter, as if holding onto them would subdue his urge. Her hips twitched, her seeping passage swelled, begging to be filled.

He jerked his gaze away, snatched a cloth from the shelf and plunged it into the kettle of warm water.

"You are to remain still," he said, more sternly than intended. But he would not explain. To say what was to come would cause grief. Better she wonder than know, for confusion would keep her alert and steady, though her arousal and his made even his own hands tremble.

He would calm. He had no choice. If he did not, he would hurt her and that was not his intent.

He twisted the cloth until it no longer dripped, then laid it over her, carefully covering all hair on her mons, labia and crease of her inner thighs.

Her gasp filled the room but he could not offer comfort, for her shock would not soon be subdued. He pressed his hand to it. Her hips jerked in response, pushing her softness into his palm. He held her still, felt the heat of her through the warmth of the cloth. Strained to think past it, to his chore and nothing more.

When his arousal and the cloth had both cooled, he dipped the cloth back into the water then pressed it to her again, preparing her for a smooth, clean inspection.

He took a candle from the shelf, settled it on the table at the crook of her inner thigh and set the cloth aside. He took in her naked beauty and though his cock still strained against his breeches, he knew his reward, as hers, would not come until her innocence had been proved.

He picked up the large warmed vial and drizzled its heavy unscented oil over her moist hairs, thickening them slightly. Then, quickly, so as not to confuse her or tease himself, he massaged the oil in further, spreading it to the root, using three fingers to rub briskly along her mons, her labia. Her hips flexed and rolled, beneath his touch. Her soft whimpers were short, shocked, and ended with a gasp and a sigh. Though he understood, it was not permitted.

"If you move further…" He reached for the sharpened blade. "…blood will be drawn."

He sat on the stool before her, leaned in, his face a teasing breath from her sweetest spot. Resting his forearm against her inner thigh, he touched the blade's edge to her flesh.

"If there be marks here…" With slow careful flicks of his wrist, he whisked away the first few hairs. "…I will know you hide not a smudge, but a curse." He used the fingertips of his free hand to flatten and pull her flesh taut, carefully shaving only the hair, leaving her sensitive flesh unharmed.

He worked silently, hearing only the crackle from the hearth, her ragged breaths and the scrape of the blade against her skin. Her scent mingled with the fragrant oil coating her body, nearly overpowered it, distracting him several times.

He leaned in closer, let the scent of the oil fill him, and remembered his task. Pulling her flesh taut, breathing through his arousal as he shaved the area where her inner thigh met that soft tender flesh beside her labia. He paused several times as waves of need pulsed through him. He forced himself to slow and fought for a more controlled and steady hand. He would not, could not, allow her beauty or soft sighs to distract him.

When finally that area was bare, he turned all attention to the other side, carefully shaving from her thigh toward her core. As he worked, his strokes became longer, steadier. Torturously slow, yet precise.

Her legs gave an occasional tremble, her belly quivered. Each time, he lifted the blade and sat back with a long bracing breath, then leaned in and started again. At last, she was bare everywhere but the edges of those sweet swollen lips, and he warned her again not to move.

"The blade is most sharp," he said as he gave it a swish in the now tepid water.

With thumb and forefinger, he stretched the first delicate lip. She gasped and his cock twitched in response. Breathing through his arousal, he scraped over her most gently. Slowly, skillfully, cutting barely three hairs at one time until none were left.

He sat back for a brief moment, then started on the other side, stretching and molding her until every hair was removed from there as well.

He shifted the candle at the crook of her thigh, bringing it closer, needing better light before shaving the next spot. With fingers pointing down, he pressed his palm to her freshly bared mound. She whimpered and tensed in response.

"Do not move." His longer fingers spread the sweet swells of her rump, allowing him access to the soft fine hairs around that tight tender bud he had tested before. He worked carefully, admonishing her several more times for shifting so restlessly while he held the blade so close.

Satisfied with his work, he set the blade safely on the ledge. Breathing deeply, he poured a small bit of thick oil into his hands, then rubbed it gently over the entire shaved area, soothing her irritated flesh. Gently, he took her now-naked lips between his oiled thumbs and forefingers, and slowly smoothed them over her, starting where they joined above her swollen hood to where they gaped wide and inviting. He searched for something that should not be but felt only ripe, wet need.

He squeezed her lips lightly, enjoyed the supple feel of them between his fingers. And then he tugged them lightly, stretching them slightly and rolled his fingers over them.

Spurred on by her soft moan, he opened them, spreading them wide. Wider. And there, nestled between those perfect pink lips was the source of both sin and ecstasy. He dared not touch it yet, certain he would not stop, though the urge to do so teased him until the need to fill her tight weeping passage had his whole body stiff and trembling.

She quivered, her juices glistened in the candlelight. And he ached. No longer able to resist, he held her open with one hand and skimmed a finger over her wet slit, from hood to hole. She gasped, bucked, and he brought his finger to his face, inhaled her tangy scent.

His cock pulsed, twitched. An invisible fist tightened around his scrotum, sending waves of agonizing pleasure coursing through him.

He closed his eyes. Breathed deeply. Slowly. Beating back the responses from his own body.

Then, with control barely regained, he leaned into her once more, touching her again, checking for any mark, any lump, anything that should not be there. He smoothed an oiled thumb down to her perineum, kneaded it gently. Her thighs trembled, her hips jerked and writhed. Her responses were expected, required, though he feared they would bring seed surging from the head of his engorged and throbbing cock.

When passion lifted her hips from the table, he dropped his hand from her. Her breaths came as rapid as his. Her hips rocked as if she sought his touch. To subdue her ache and his, he had only to release himself from the constraint of his breeches…

He pinched her lips closed, allowed her sudden jolt of movement, did not hush her when she cried out.

He stood quickly, grabbed the now cool, damp cloth and wiped it over her freshly shaven mound and inner thighs, removing loose hairs and excess oil. He swiped it over the table, then tossed it to the floor and set the kettle beside the legs of the stool.

Drawing another deep breath, he snatched the vial of thick oil and he sat before her inveigling sweetness once more, eager to complete this final inspection and prove what he believed to be true. Only then, would he see to her needs and his.

Though it should be slow and gentle, he knew without question their joining would be quick, for surely their first flood of passion would come fast and hard.

Chapter Six

He touched her still, coating warm oil over her like a salve upon her tender flesh. Nothing existed but the feelings of hot need he awakened within her womb.

His fingers, as he molded her nether lips for the blade, were like irons made to brand her. The heat, the rough scraping, his skillful touches -the sound of her own shuddering breaths - stirred her, and she feared passion might shatter her as he sat between her spread legs, watching. Even the cool wet cloth he wiped over her failed to subdue her need.

And then he parted her lips and tipped the amber vial until more of that thick oil slid over her, teasing her, like a feather against her. Awakening every nerve, every exposed bit of her. His fingers followed, slippery against her craving flesh.

Her eyes clenched shut and a moan escaped her though she tried to hold it back. He uttered a small groan of his own and she opened her eyes just enough to look down to where he sat.

His intense gaze grew as needy as her body, and for a moment she wished he would lay with her, take her, let her feel what it was like to be filled with more than her own fingers, to be taken to the heights of primal screams, to find release from this overwhelming ache he created.

Her face grew hot as images of him taking her tormented her mind the same as his fingers tormented her body.

He sat back but did not remove his hands from her. And then he closed his eyes and a breath hissed through his teeth. When he opened his eyes again, his desire was gone and a hard, distant look took its place.

He moved the candle at her thigh and leaned in closer to her core. She could no longer see his eyes, just the thick dark hair on his head. But his fingers…his thumbs… were on her, palpating her thick lips. Brushing her sensitive inner lips. Flicking them. Smoothing lower to tease the entrance of her wet passage. Tension curled her toes and tightened her shaky thighs. Her world was his touch and the liquid heat that dripped from her.

He spread his fingers apart, opening her.

With a strangled cry of yearning, she pulled at the ties on her wrists, desperate to make him stop, but he did not. He spread her yet wider and dipped the tips of his thumbs inside. Her heels pressed to the table and her back arched, her body little more than a writhing heap of throbbing need. She tensed, tried to drop her knees, to close him out, to not let passion claim her for she barely had the strength of will to fight it.

"Do not move," he said, his voice thick as his thumbs pulsed against the entrance, as if hoping to pry it open further. "I will see more of you."

More of her? He spoke of her maidenhead, of that she was sure. If he had not noticed before, he would notice now. Would he think her purity was lost to a man… a boy… or the beast? Surely he would not believe if she told him the truth…

He would now test her somehow. As proof she had not lain with evil, he would make her feel pain. Would scold her, accuse her. Punish her.

She held her breath, feared his rage. Had caught a mere glimpse of it when he saw the mark in the mirror. He would have beaten her if doubt had not stopped him.

His fingers shifted, no longer inside the edge of her yet stretching her just the same, as if he held her open with the fingers of one hand. And then she felt heat. More intense than his touch. It was a steady building sensation, burning her as if…

Sudden panic filled her and she lifted her head, looked down at him as he held the candle's flame yet closer to her, and closer still, even as his fingers her spread her.

No!

She thought of the whispered accounts of tormented witches. Of them being burned. Of pins being thrust inside of them.

He would do the same to her, believing her tainted. A witch's womb was the source of shame, of evil, for if she had lain with the beast, it was a most unnatural joining. If he believed in her guilt, he would sear her flesh, stick her with pins, deform her so no one would ever want her, touch her, not even the devil himself.

Tremors of terror wracked her body. She was at his mercy, his fingers urging her open, making her need, thrusting her from passion to panic. She could not block his touch, his branding. Yet she could not bear it.

"Abigail?"

Her rapid breaths made her dizzy, but she struggled on. Strained at the ties that held her in place as tears slid unchecked from her eyes. Sobs wrenched themselves from her tight, dry throat.

"Abigail!"

The heat subsided and then he was beside her. His hot hand smoothing her hair from her forehead. Another resting below her breast. She turned away from his questioning eyes, tried to bury her face in her raised arm. Breathed hard and heavy as tears fell and fear wedged itself deeper inside of her.

His hand left her rib. His fingers clasped her jaw, and he turned her face toward his. "What do you fear?"

She clenched her eyes shut, was unable to give voice to her thoughts, unable to block them from her mind.

His fingers tightened on her jaw. "You will look at me."

She opened her eyes.

"Why do you weep?" His gaze turned hard. "What do you hide?"

"I cannot hide!" She cried openly. Tried to pull from his grasp. Whimpered when she could not. He released her and she rocked her head side to side. "You see all of me. You touch all of me… I yield to it… but please… I beg you…do not stick me, do not burn me."

His hand on her forehead was gentle, brushing over her slowly, tenderly. "What is this plea?" His other hand claimed her breast. Covered it, kneaded it. Rubbed circles over her nipple until staggering need returned to her again. He released her breast. Gripped the candle and held it for her to see. "Is it this you fear?"

She stared at the flame as it hovered above her breasts. How many witches were burned – for confessions, for punishment?

"You will answer."

"I…" She pressed the tears from her eyes, then looked up at him, blinking when more tears surfaced. The fury and accusation she expected were absent from his voice and from his eyes. Did he not believe in her guilt? "I… have heard…"

"No one is to speak of their time in this room." He set the candle down. "What have you heard?"

"Whispers."

His gaze did not leave hers but rather probed as if pulling the answer from her.

"That witches are burned," she said, "and pricked with pins until their screams fall silent."

"Witches."

"Yes."

"Are you a witch, Abigail?"

She was presumed guilty until proven so, as were all the accused. To deny it would mean torture. To confess it would mean death. "Would a witch submit to this shameful baring?" She tugged at the restraints for emphasis. "Would she submit to this arduous testing?"

He looked as if her questions were not new to his ears. "A witch can bear much testing."

She shook her head, set her gaze firmly on his, wished for him to look nowhere but her eyes. To see her as more than a clump of flesh to poke and prod. To believe she was untouched by the dark one. "But it is not only the witch..." Her voice was like that of a prayer. Breathless. Impassioned. "…it is the accused, as well, who have endured such treatment…"

His hand stilled on her forehead. "Have I harmed you?"

He had whipped her and probed her. Somehow stirring her with every touch, soothing her, even declaring a want to prove her innocence. Perhaps his mind was still convinced though his eyes had told him otherwise.

"I have... felt pain this hour."

He squeezed her breast, making her gasp. "Some pain must be felt." His grip tightened and she whimpered. "Yet too much can numb the body and the mind." He loosened his hold. "That is not my intent. I want you to feel…" He kneaded her gently. "Do you feel, Abigail?" His palm smoothed over her nipple, creating a tingling friction she felt through to her toes. "Do you feel my touch?"

"I do…"

"Did you feel the crop as it struck your breasts…your nipples?" His gaze locked on hers as he pinched her nipple then pulsed his fingers to it, rhythmically milking pleasure from it.

Voiceless, she nodded.

He tipped his face closer to her, as he milked the other nipple. Back and forth he went, one breast to the other, pinching, pulsing. Triggering sparks of pain and dizzying pleasure. "Did you feel the heat of shame as you bent over this table and felt my finger enter you?"

She felt it then as now. Hot stinging shame. And he knew. Had expected it, though she hoped he would not know how many feelings that vulgar touch awakened within her. Feelings of want and of need, as well as shame.

"Did you feel the slow stretch of your muscles as they surrendered… when, given your will, you would have resisted?"

She nodded as he spoke, her eyes on his, his voice lulling her into a trance, his hands keeping her alert and on edge.

He palmed her breast, gently kneaded it again, then let go and touched his fingertips to her mouth, brushing over her lips, parting them. "Did cries of pleasure not escape these lips as I spread oil onto your pubis? And as I removed the hair veiling your lovely treasures?"

Her reply was a moan against his fingers as he dipped three of them into her mouth, pulsed them over her tongue, withdrew them, then did it again, slowly, inching them in further, widening her jaw as the tips of them nearly reached her throat, soaking them, making her crave. He withdrew them again, then smoothed their wetness over her nipples, mingling it with the oil still on her flesh from when he helped her massage it on, the slick smooth feeling making her back arch, her eyes grow heavy, her legs quiver.

"You see?" he said as he glided his hand down over her oiled ribs to her belly. "Pain is merely one way to draw a response." He palmed her core, making her whimper. Yet his gaze never left hers and she was forced to look into his eyes, to let him see how responsive he had made her mind and her body. "Do you feel my touch, Abigail? Do you fear it still?"

"I feel it…" The words came out on a sigh.

"And do you fear it?"

How could she not? Every stroke of his fingers over her wet swollen lips, every heated caress, brought her to a new height, a new flood of need and warmth.

"I... do not know." She arched her hips, trying to press her core to his palm, wanting, needing more, even as shame scorched her face.

But he did not oblige, and as her hips rose to him, he pulled his hot hand away. Leaving her cold and aching.

"There is real pain," he said, "and the perception of pain." He feathered his fingertips over her belly in slow, mesmerizing circles. "Nothing this hour has brought more pain than you can withstand." He reached for the candle. "Nor will it." Lifted it from the table. "That is my word." Held it high above her breasts. "Do you accept my word?"

Her gaze shifted from the intensity of his to the burning candle he held above her.

"I will hear your answer."

Her gaze shot back to his. "I...do."

He tipped the candle, sending drops of hot wax onto her breast. With a scream, she bucked, tried to shake it off as the heat of it grew more intense. It slowly faded and the wax hardened against her like another layer of skin.

He tipped the candle again, over her nipple. The hot wax coating it. She screamed again, her back arching, her head rolling side to side as the wax turned from hot to hotter, then cooled and grew thick and solid.

He held it over her other nipple, captured her gaze as the hot wax hit her. She cried out again, her nipples so tender, so awake and alive. The weight of the hardening wax on them an agonizing pleasure that rippled straight to her spread and throbbing core.

He waved the candle over her, let several drops land between her breasts, not pausing as he trailed them lower, over her ribs and her belly, turning her gasps into one long-held breath.

He dripped more over each thigh. Some of it hardened on impact, some was so hot it felt cold as it cascaded down her inner thighs and dried in ribbons that tightened like fingers against her. Each drop drew a muffled cry from her throat, made her writhe and strain at the ties holding her open to him. And then he went to the foot of the table, locked his gaze on hers and raised the candle a full arm's length over her shaved mons.

Her eyes widened as understanding dawned, and she shook her head slowly. Silently begging.

And then his fingers were on those nether lips, parting them again and though she tried to scream a plea, only a breath - harsh and moist - escaped her. He lifted his gaze to the flame, raised his arm a tad higher, then looked down to where he held her open.

He tipped the candle again.

The hot wax fell on her throbbing nub, it strangled her cries, made her body quake, as if the tremors might cool it faster. Heat pulsed through her as it sealed that bit of her in a hot cocoon. It seemed to swell even as the wax cooled and thickened around it. And then he pinched her nether lips closed, securing the wax to her. Locking in the warmth though it did not burn, it aroused, it squeezed there as on her nipples, making her yet more aware of it.

He lowered the candle, looked at her over the flame. Then snuffed it with his fingertips. "Was it as you feared?" His voice was gruff. Forced and breathy.

She had feared the heat as it hit her and grew. And then it subsided and pleasure replaced the pain. Still, her heart hammered hard against her ribs, her breathing was ragged and her body craved and quivered.

"It was..." Her sheathed nub throbbed, seemed to fight for release from the hardened wax. "...bearable." Even her words trembled. "Please... has it yet proven my innocence?"

He shook his head slowly. "There is more," he said as he poured oil from the large vial into his hand then worked it carefully over the candle's fat end.

Though he barely glanced at her eyes as he oiled the candle, he knew she looked at him in earnest, seeking to please, afraid what pleasing might entail. So was the impressive strength of her resolve. She was unlike any other. Even through her terror, she had yielded. She did not require the pricking test. Nor did she require a severe whip of the crop, the bite of clamps or the drowning test.

Her body responded and her mind was keen, and though her cries made him fear he had hurt her, he feared more that she might have been soon to confess. The ache of those thoughts affected his heart as powerfully as her sighs affected his cock.

He would not frighten her further. He would not inspect her by light of the candle, would not search beyond her torn maidenhead for a mark of the beast within her deepest recess. Instead, he would gauge sensations inside of her.

He set the oiled candle on her belly then ran his long oiled fingers over her labia, felt their fullness, saw only her moist beauty. He grazed his fingertip over her slit, her inner lips, oiling her. Her legs quivered and he understood. She felt his every touch and ached as much as he.

He flattened his palms against her, smoothed his hands back, spreading her lips wide, like the splitting of a fragrant and succulent fruit. He spread her wider still, stretching her tiny hood, exposing her wax-coated nub once again.

Holding her open with the fingers of one hand, he drizzled the thick oil over her, then smoothed his fingertips lower to spread her tiny passage wider, preparing it.

He grabbed the candle then pried his eyes away from her body and looked into hers. Without speaking, he settled the fat end against her sweet hole. Her brows furrowed, her eyes showed fear. A low moan, like that of awareness and need, came from her and he could take no more. Still holding her open, he dropped his gaze and eased the end of the candle into her, watching as her hungry wetness welcomed it inside.

Her sharp gasps and sudden stillness stirred him. She sounded surprised by the sensations, as if they were all new to her, though he knew from the breach, not all of them were. But he was the examiner, not her almighty judge, and though others may have had her before, he would prove the beast had not been among them.

He gave the candle a half turn. Her belly tensed, her breathing became more labored. And then he pulled it out, pleased by her reactions so far.

"If you are untouched," he said, "you will feel when I stop moving it into you." He worked the candle back in, slowly, gradually, barely a knuckle's depth. Then two. Three. Imagining the burgeoning head of his cock in its place and disappearing inside of her. He pulled it out of her. "You will then tighten yourself around it…" He pushed it back in, this time further. "…and hold it within." Then he slowly, almost imperceptibly, pumped it within her.

Her breath hitched and her back arched and though she closed her eyes, he did not reprimand her.

And then he stopped moving it and let his fist lightly circle its tapered end. It shifted against his palm as her body clenched around it, proving to his utter satisfaction that the devil had not touched this most secret and precious bit of her.

He pulled the candle out slightly then stopped, and she clenched again, making him swell with thoughts of how tight her passage was for the candle, a mere fraction of his size, and how snug she would be around him. He pushed it back in, a full fist's length, her gasp sending a hard spasm through him.

"Hold tightly," he said, letting go of it. "Do not let it fall."

He wanted to rip it out of her and toss it to the floor, then plunge himself inside of her and feel those tight muscles gripping him. He would make her back arch further. He would make her contort in ways only pleasure could educe, not in some withering maniacal way as would be if she had lain with the beast.

But to ignite her passionate flames further, with her senses so heightened, would bring her too soon to the brink. Her examination had lasted a near hour, she was worthy of the same in pleasure, free from fear.

He looked over her tense body, from her open mouth, her heaving breasts and the wax coating her nipples, like small prisons from which he knew they ached for release. And he would release them. He glanced at the blade on the shelf and considered warning her. But then the candle shifted as her body again shuddered, and he feared she might reach the brink without aid.

"You will open your eyes," he said without taking his eyes from the candle, unmoving now as it protruded from her.

And her hooded nub, encased in that solid layer of wax… he imagined the feel of the casing as if it coated his cock, as if his cock had to strain against that thick hard layer the way it strained against the confines of his breeches. Though her nub was so concealed, it beseeched him as if his fingers still spread her, baring it merely for his pleasure.

He felt the heat of her gaze, steady on him as he looked at her sex. If he could find his voice, he would tell her she was innocent. That she had pleased him in ways he could not express.

He reached for the blade on the shelf. It glinted in the candlelight as he flattened it to the wax on her thigh. She flinched as the first bit of wax lifted from her flesh. He peeled it off with his fingers then scraped the blade beneath the next bit and peeled that off as well.

With every scratch against her, she responded fully, writhing as the sensations stirred her. Not once did she not react when she should have. And then he stood by her breasts and flattened the flesh so he could press the blade beneath the wax.

Ever so slowly he peeled it from first one nipple and then the other. Her sighs and shocked gasps filled the air, reaching him like a caress against his own engorged arousal.

He ran his hands over her body as the wax was removed, revelled in the silky feel of her, the softness, the tension of her muscles as they quivered beneath his palm.

He stood at her hip and reached for the candle, then slowly turned it inside of her again. Her breaths came quick and loud. Her belly tightened. Her charms where there for him to enjoy, to touch and smell and taste. He needed only to secure her consent.

He rounded the end of the table and stood between her legs. Only the wax on her core remained. He set the blade on the shelf then spread her lips with his fingers and carefully stripped the wax away, leaving her red, swollen. Beautiful.

He pulled the candle out in one move, watching her body quiver as though seeking to take it inside of her again. He set it aside. "You have done well," he said and smoothed his palms over her spread thighs, relieved to know that lovely Abigail, though not untouched, did not carry the mark of the beast.

He rounded the table again, and released the ties at her wrists.

Her eyes were wide and steady on his. "I... am free?"

He lowered one of her arms, rubbed her shoulder and neck, working his fingertips into her stiff muscles, feeling them soften beneath his touch. "You are as I hoped." He lowered her other arm, rubbed it the same. "Unmarked."

A tear slipped from her eye as a slight smile tugged at her lips. His own smile began to form then faded with hers. He brushed her tear with his finger as the pained expression of need grew in her eyes.

He leaned closer, his lips a breath from her ear. "What is it you seek, Abigail?"

"I…do not know."

"You do," he whispered, "and you need not fear the words." Straightening, he skimmed his hand down over her belly, and snuggled his fingers between her still-swollen lips. "If it is this you crave..." he pulsed his fingers against her. "...you may say it."

She moaned softly. "Good Sir... I…" Her words fell away as her head rocked side to side.

"Or is it more of this…" He slid a finger, slick with her juices, deep inside of her.

Her body trembled, her eyes closed. "I am your most humble servant… " she said on a breath, her face aflame. "I accept that which you offer."

Mayhap she was a witch because she bewitched him as no other. "No, Abigail." His voice sounded foreign to his own ears. It was thick and raspy. "For this moment, I bow to your wish. You need only speak it.

"I ache." Her eyes fluttered open, her gaze locked on his. "Because of your touch... and yet..."

He slid a second finger inside of her. "Do you want more of my touch, Abigail?"

She sucked in a halting breath, released it with the words, "I...do."

Without removing his fingers from her, he leaned into her again, and touched his lips to hers, gently parting them with his own until his tongue swirled over hers.

He would take this slowly, would grant her full pleasure, for he had nearly condemned her when he saw the smudge. She had earned release and he owed her for that fear.

He sealed the kiss, brushed his lips against hers. Felt her warm breath against his face and gazed down at her softly closed eyes. Then slowly, with absolute control, he eased his fingers further inside of her. Her hips pulsed against him and he held still, letting her express the enormity of her need.

He withdrew his fingers without warning, then, on her gasp, plunged them back in. There was no resistance. He withdrew them again, then plunged three inside of her and her hips rose to meet them. He was eager to have her, eager to plunge his cock into her, imagined her hot wet need encompassing him, gripping him, helping him reach the release he had ached for since first seeing her tied and spread in the yard, her beautiful breasts bared before him.

He eased his fingers from her, resisted the desire to bring them to his lips so he could taste her.

Her eagerness was as heady as his. Her scent, stronger now that he permitted himself to revel in it. It drew him back to the table's end, and as he made his way there, he feathered his fingertips over her belly, barely touching her, simply grazing the surface. Watching her body writhe in response.

He dusted his fingers over her hip and that sensitive spot where it met her thigh. And then he leaned in and brushed his lips to her knee. He would make her pleasure linger if he could, but knew he could not last much longer without having her.

He reached the end of the table, untied the restraint at her ankle and smoothed his hands over her leg, kneading her calf, her knee, her thigh, then working the stiffness from her hip. And then he released the other restraint and soothed those muscles the same.

He had acquired her consent but it was not enough. He wanted her to open to him, to submit freely, fully. And though their first joining would take them each beyond reason, beyond sense, it would not quench their desire. He would arouse her again, take her slowly the second time, giving her the gift of heightened pleasure after all the fear and pain she had endured.

He poured oil into his palms, warmed it in his hands, then smoothed it over her legs, her hips. She sighed and trembled, her body dimpled where he did not touch.

He dipped his head and inhaled the moist fragrant heat rising from her body like invisible fingers reaching out to him, drawing him closer. He thought to lift her from the table, to carry her to the hearth and lay her before its warmth, to let his hands roam her whole body and awaken her every nerve.

She whispered a plea, a soft breathy coo of words he could not discern, and then her legs eased open for him, without the ties to force her.

He slid his hands over her belly, her waist and hips. "These moments are yours Abigail," he said as he drank in her eager wetness, glistening there before him.

At her soft sigh, he smoothed his palms along her inner thighs, enjoying how each caress made her body tremble. He smoothed them over her again, bringing them closer to her core, letting his thumbs brush over her.

A shudder rippled through her. A sigh, more like a moan, escaped her lips. And he could take no more. He released his throbbing cock from the confines of his breeches then captured it in his oiled palm, coating the head and the veiny, bulging shaft until it swelled well beyond the point of comfort.

He grasped her outer thighs and lifted her legs, holding them at his hips as he pressed his aching, needy head into her. Her body convulsed then swallowed it greedily, and then reason was lost and he plunged all the way in, his pelvis smashing into hers.

She screamed, a sharp cry of shock and pain. Like that of a maiden.

Body and mind in battle, he stilled. Stared at her. Swallowed the crescendo of yearning within him. Saw pain in her eyes, on her face…

But it could not be. It should not be, for he had not taken her innocence. He looked down at their joining, his cock buried within her, the base enveloped within her full wet folds.

What was this trickery? Purity by deception? If she feigned pain now, mayhap she had feigned both pain and pleasure before.

Fury tightened his hands on her thighs until she cried out. And still he held tight, willing his pulsing cock to calm.

He set his gaze on her face – her eyes clenched, her brows still bunched – and he breathed through his need, slowly easing himself from her, fighting the friction, aching to hold on, to not spend his seed. Unwilling to open himself further to the evil that lay within her. For if she had lain with the beast, it would still reside there and, by this mating, might now also lie within him.

The sheer force of his entry shocked her. It ripped the air from her lungs, while the size of him kept her immobile until she was sure she was not torn in two. And then he held himself against her. His body pressing her aching core, arousing her past the pain of that first thrust, pushing her need higher until she feared she might burst from the pressure. The tingling warmth once created by her own fingers was nothing compared to the insatiable heat and hunger she felt as he filled her.

He shifted, and the sensations within her grew. The slight movement of his body, starting to pull from hers, made her long to draw him back in.

She opened her eyes, looked into his, started when she saw the fierce intensity there. Wondered if need showed as plainly on her face as his.

And then he eased further from her, his body no longer pressing against hers. Everything inside of her screamed for him to return, to fill her once more, to pierce her with his searing warmth.

As if on their own, her muscles contracted, tightening around him as they had on the candle.

His eyes clenched shut and he tipped his head back as if beseeching something from above. The thick passion of him throbbed inside of her, aroused her in ways she did not fully understand. He had said this moment was hers, but she knew not what to do, how to quench this need.

He pulled back a fraction more. She tightened her grip on him, held him deep within her, and a breath hissed from him. His hands squeezed her thighs, his fingertips bore into her flesh as if he meant to mark her, to leave clear proof of this mating upon her flesh. She covered his hands with hers, meant to pry his fingers from her, held on instead, needing him to finish this thing he started.

He moved again, easing back, the slight shift teasing her, making her crave and sigh.

And then he stopped all movement and stared down at her with an intensity she did not understand. The tightness of his lips, the deep crease in his brow, the hard penetrating gleam in his eyes… it was not a look of pleasure. Something had changed. Something was different but she knew not what or why. She knew only that he wore the same pained and accusing expression now as when he saw the mark on her breast through the looking glass.

"You were not untouched."

He believed her to be pure? Untouched not just by the beast…

But he had examined her. He would have seen the breach. He would know her maidenhead was not his to take…

She stared up at him, had meant no deceit. Hers was a moment of indiscretion. She should not have watched the rutting, but it was her own hand. It was never like this. No man had ever touched her as she had been touched this hour. No man had ever seen her body, made her sigh and quiver. And want.

"Never…" She shook her head slowly, pleaded with her eyes...for understanding. For forgiveness. For more of his touches.

His expression only hardened, he barely blinked, his lips paled as he held them yet tighter. And then he all but pulled out of her.

She clenched her muscles again as he moved, trying to gauge his responses now as he had gauged hers this last hour. She shifted beneath him, pitched her hips up and back until his eyes closed and she knew his passion had surged once more.

She would make him see how deeply she felt every solid bit of him. How she ached to hold him inside of her, to have him forget his doubt and to remove that look of betrayal from his face.

She relaxed her muscles, then clenched them again and he trembled, groaned, turned his face to the side, closed his eyes as if he struggled with the feelings as much as she. This brief moment of mastery she held over him aroused her as much as the fullness of him. The heat.

His hips rocked against her again, a slow movement that grew in intensity until his arousal pumped within her, once, twice, three times, creating a new tension that stole her breath. And then he stopped and her back arched as if on its own, her head lolled back.

She reached for him, silently begging him to sooth her ache, to touch her with his fingers, to move again, faster, harder. To satisfy the need he caused with his every tormenting thrust.

He did not respond to that need.

She moved against him, lifted her hips. His low moan, the rush of his inhaled breath as he held firm and still within her… told of the power she held in this moment. She made him ache, made him need and want. He would remember this feeling, as would she. He would forget her impurity, and recall how she had felt his every touch upon and within her body. And how he felt her every touch upon his. She tightened around him again.

A growl rumbled through his entire body and he slammed into her with exquisite power, his pelvis solid against hers. Pulsing violently as a rush of warmth gushed into her.

Tension and need shook her body as his seed spilled into her. Her lungs ached as she gulped in air. Her womb grasped at him, eager for something more than this fullness. For something just out of reach…

And then she was empty. Cold. Dripping. Grasping at him as he stood back, his eyes dark with anger she did not understand. She felt fear, yet her body still craved. She wanted him inside of her again, wanted him pressed against her.

She reached for him, silently pleading, but he stood back further, breaking all contact except for his gaze, now locked on hers as if he could not look away.

"I ache." The words rushed past her lips like a plea. He said these moments were hers… She had but to ask. "Please…"

"You have deceived me." He adjusted his breeches, securing himself inside of them.

She gasped at the pain in his whispered words. She had submitted. Had allowed herself to be aroused by his hands, to be shamed and marked by the crop. Allowed him to see her every secret spot, even the breach. She did all this to convince him of her innocence, to have him see her as untouched by the beast not by man, to forget the smudge upon the mirror. And she had, until this moment.

She sat up. Felt an overwhelming need to cover herself as he stood there, fully clothed and fuming. She draped an arm across her breasts, settled a hand in her lap. "You saw all of me. I could not hide –"

"You were not untouched, yet you cried out, pretending to feel pain you should not feel."

She shook her head, unable to answer this accusation. She did feel pain. Was unprepared for his size, his strength.

He charged at her and she raised her hands to shield herself from his advance. He snatched her by the arms. His fury, sudden movement and tight grip brought tears to her eyes.

"Was it the same with the crop?" He spoke as if he feared the words. "Pretend?"

She shook her head again, slowly, stunned by his accusations. "No." She had felt every strike.

"With the wax and with my touch?" His voice grew thicker, lower, as if each word brought him new certainty. "What cries were true? What sighs feigned?"

She could not stop the tears. "I have not deceived." She feared him now, had nothing left to offer, no proof left to give. She had felt the pain and the pleasure… how could he not believe? "I felt it all."

His fingers tightened on her arms. "Only dalliance with the devil would prompt trickery to mark me as well."

Understanding came to her with vicious clarity. Despite her shame this hour, her cries and her sighs, he no longer believed her untouched by the beast, and when a man spills his seed within a witch, the devil may then reside within him…

She raised trembling hands to his chest. He flinched before she could reach him, and she dropped her hands to her lap. "You are not marked." Her voice was weak, the words hollow.

He released her roughly, stood back, his hands in fists at his sides. "Confess your deception now or I will wrest it from you."

Anger merged with the fear inside of her. She had withstood his examination with all his prodding. Her body was welted and bruised. She yielded completely to both gentleness and force.

"When a woman is accused, she is dishonored," she said, blinking tears of shame and fury from her eyes. "She is bared and shaved." Her entire body trembled. The sensation made her want to run. To scream. Instead she sat tall, clasped her palms to the edge of the table and fixed her gaze on his. "She is beaten and probed and aroused past shame."

She thought of all he did to her. Of how she sat there naked before him. How he controlled her every thought, watched her every response. How he offered a mere moment of pleasure for all the torment he inflicted. And how he ripped it away without providing for her, his suspicions high as he now feared for himself, as if bedding her had marked his own soul.

Drawing a slow choppy breath, she let her gaze drift over him, then lifted her chin and forced the rest of the words past her lips. "How, Good Sir, would an accused be examined if it be not a woman…" She locked her gaze on his. "…but a man?"

With the speed of a sprite, he reached out, snatched her arm and dragged her from the tabletop. She landed hard on her bare feet then stumbled after him as he rounded the table, regretting her words and her tone.

"Forgive!" She pleaded through tears as terror filled her. "Please! I felt it all…" He would condemn her now, toss her to the crowd and proclaim her marked. "Please… forgive."

He flung her from his grip and her rump hit the table's wide edge. "You will not move," he said then turned his back to her.

She struggled to catch her breath as she rubbed her arm, only to shudder violently as he stormed over to that horrid chest with its assortment of hideous devices. She dared not look at them overlong earlier when she did his bidding and retrieved the amber vials from it. But there were needles inside of it. Crops of differing sizes, a vicious iron claw, wrapped bundles of items she dared not imagine…

He knelt before it, reached in and though she willed her legs to move, to take her from this place, she knew there was no place safe for her to go.

"Please, Good Sir, I beg you..."

ଓଃ

He would not listen to her pleas, would not be moved by her tears, her cries, her scent.

He would test her again, every bit of her, without the care and restraint he had shown her before. And he would prove her innocence, whatever it took, pain or pleasure. He must, for if she proved to be marked, he would be condemned as well.

He grabbed the pins in his fist. Felt the weight of them. Thought of her tender flesh and how desperately she begged not to be burned or pierced. Many feared the pricking test but none had sobbed in terror at the thought of it. He dropped them, unsure why her fear still mattered to him.

He grabbed for the more cruel devices left by governors before. One by one, he flung them to the far side of the chest. There were other ways to prove innocence and other means by which to acquire confessions. Ways that intimidated, frightened, but did not disfigure.

He reached into the bottom of the chest and grabbed the large, heavy sack that held the items he needed. A plug much thicker than his pinky, metal clamps, and a stone phallus beyond his girth.

"Please."

He looked at her as she stared at him, eyes wide and wet. He turned away, not willing to be moved by the fear he saw there.

"You will turn your back," he said, his eyes averted from hers.

It took her as long to turn as for him to reach her. He set the bundle beside her on the table. The clunk of the phallus, the harsh metal clang of the clamps and her hard heavy breaths, were loud in the thickly silent room.

He opened the bundle, set the items aside and rolled the cloth into a long, wide strip.

He covered her eyes with it, tying the ends behind her head, ignoring the way small whimpers shook her body, the way her tears wet the cloth.

Choice was not his, she had forced this action. He would not be deceived again. If she could not see, she could not anticipate his touch or adjust her responses. To fully test her, to note how she would respond to pain versus pleasure, he would keep her sightless and vary the sensations, create confusion so she could not pretend.

"Turn once more."

She slowly turned to face him, her head down. He snatched her chin with his fingers, lifted it, made sure her eyes were fully covered, then broke the contact.

Her ragged breaths jostled her breasts. Her nipples were stiff and still red from the hot wax. Could she have feigned those responses? The gasps and sighs so precise? He could not risk it, for, in truth, he knew not whether she had lain with the beast, nor if he, too, was now marked.

He grabbed her nipples between his fingers, pinched them, felt a moment of regret when she cried out. But test her he must.

He released one and reached for a clamp. "Lock your hands behind you," he said. "Do not let go."

Chapter Nine

His hands were rough on her breasts, squeezing, pinching her. She cried out. And then he pinched harder.

She was at his mercy, unable to see, only to hear and feel. She would listen to everything as he tested her, would keep her senses keen. With all that was in her, every morsel of strength and hope, she would respond fully, with tears or with sighs. Despite the shame. Despite the pain. Though if he were to use the cruel devices within his reach she would crumble and say whatever words he would believe. And that confession could damn them both.

Sniffing back fear and confusion, she did as he ordered and clasped her trembling hands behind her.

He gripped her nipple tighter, as if all of his fingers closed over it, and pulled. She whimpered, unable to remain silent, but did not pull from his grasp. Then a horrible sound, like that of irons, assailed her senses.

Shackles? She lost her breath to a sudden surge of panic. Would he send her back into the forest? Leave her there until dawn, like others before her? Naked and open to the elements, the animals and the villagers…

Tears pooled behind the blinder then slipped through as she silently begged him to spare her such cruelty.

"You weep for yourself, not for those harmed by your deception." His voice was hard, gruff. Yet his fingers gentled on her nipple, lightly rubbed it between his fingers. She felt it stiffen, peak, as though it reached out to him for more.

She breathed deeply. Unsure whether he meant his touch to be tender or cruel. And then his fingers wrapped around her breast, gripping it from the side, and the sound of irons assailed her once again.

"What do you feel?" he asked.

She felt confused, frightened. She opened her mouth to say so when something hard and cold captured her nipple, sending a sharp bolt of pain through her breast as if teeth made of iron nibbled it. Sounds came from her but words would not form. Her nipple throbbed, so hard, so fierce, she thought it might dislodge the iron clamp.

"You will answer," he said, and clamped her other nipple.

"Heat!" The word came out with a sob of shock. Her hands slipped from her own grip and she jerked them behind her again, clasped them. The movement jostled the clamps, made them sway and bob as they tugged her sensitive flesh.

Her breaths came hard and fast as she adjusted to the sensations. The pain, like that of the crop, shocked and aroused at the same time. Her breasts felt heavy, weighted. Her nipples ached, tingled, as pulsing waves of warmth spiraled down to her core. "I feel sharp, biting heat."

He turned her around, gripped her locked hands in his fist and urged her forward. Her thighs hit the table and he pushed her down over it, flattening her aching nipples to the surface, forcing the clamps to dig into her breasts.

He nudged her feet apart with his then held her still for a breath, and she knew she was to remain in this terrible position, forced by sheer will to remain exposed, without benefit of restraints.

And then he was gone, the steady thud of his boots trailing off, taking him toward the end of the table, near the stool. Something scrapped against the wooden shelf. Was it the blade? Another candle? What method of testing would she be made to endure now?

Her breath caught in her throat and she forced herself to calm. To breathe through her fear. He had told her his intent was not to hurt her. If her responses were true and swift, he would not hurt her still, despite his anger and fear. This she would believe.

He returned to her. She clasped her hands tighter, giving him no cause to correct her.

His boots scraped and scuffed against the floor as if he took small deliberate steps within the space around her. There were other sounds, too. His breathing, as loud and ragged as her own, the rustle of his sleeve brushing his doublet. The pop of the stopper on the vial of oil…

She drew a sudden breath as understanding came to her. And then the cool thick oil dripped over her rump and between her cheeks, coating her tight rear passage.

He meant to spear her there again. The heat of that memory seared her face.

"What do you feel?" His words were dry, with an air of indifference, as if his attention had shifted elsewhere. Yet his breaths still came quick and unsteady.

Though she wished to take comfort in that hint of his arousal, she dared not ignore the dark mood that simmered beneath.

"I feel… afraid…"

His shoes scuffed the floor again, then stopped, and something solid was pressed against her. Something much larger than his finger had been. She thought to block it, to cover herself with her hands, but she dared not, and locked them more firmly together.

"You will push back."

With a low murmur of surrender, she obeyed and felt herself stretched as the hard, rounded object gained entry. She recalled his prior urgings and breathed through the fear and budding pain as he increased pressure and pushed it further into her. She forced her muscles to soften, fought against them each time they tensed.

Then all pressure stopped and the oil coated her once more, as if he poured it onto her in a steady stream. It warmed as it drizzled between her cheeks and pooled at her filled and overstretched hole. Then it slid beyond, slow and thick, gliding over her nether lips, teasing them, mingling with his seed that still clung to her.

The pressure grew again as he pushed the smooth object further inside of her, cold bit by cold bit. Stretching her. Filling her. Arousing her.

She drew a long slow breath and gave into the sensations. She could not fight them, could not fight him. He would do to her as he pleased, and she could not, would not, resist. She swallowed useless tears of shame as he pushed it in yet further. Slowly, barely moving it as if he meant for her to feel every bit of its length and its width. Her breaths came in heavy pants, her hands, gripped tightly to each other, ached. And still he filled her.

"What do you feel?"

"I feel… full," she said, aware of the breathless tone of her voice, wondered if he noticed it too.

Her muscles clenched as the filling went on and she pushed back, relaxed her muscles and breathed fully, allowing it deep inside. The pressure stopped yet the fullness lingered.

"You will stand." The gentleness of his tone softened the shock of his words.

How could she stand while impaled this way? She drew a breath, unsure if she could move. And then his fingers closed over her upper arms and he eased her upright. Held her back against him for a brief moment.

She breathed slowly. Felt the hard buttons of his doublet pressed to her spine, the heat of his solid chest behind her, his arousal against the probe wedged inside of her. Every breath she took, every quiver of her body, made her yet more aware of it. Part of it pressed outside of her body, as if its base held her cheeks apart, purposely exposing her, displaying how thoroughly she had been filled.

The clamps dangled heavily from her breasts, pulled on her nipples, elongating them. The sensations merged with those of his hands and his heat, creating confusing curls of need deep within her.

He let go of her suddenly and she felt cold. Unsteady.

"Turn." His voice was dry, raspy. As if frustrated by his own pleasure.

She shifted slowly, blindly. Every step made the clamps sway and seemed to stretch her tight hole further. Awareness centered on those feelings, distracting her, and she knew not where he stood or whether she yet faced him. She paused, listened. Heard his breathing and took a final awkward step. She gasped as her breasts bobbed and her nipples grew cold and needy.

His breath hitched as if he felt the same shocking sensations as she. She thought to ask if he did, to make him say what he felt, for she knew he could not deny his own arousal. He feared the mark, but were his responses, like hers, not proof he was untouched? Surely he knew there was no need to test her further.

She drew a desperate breath, eager for this to end. "I have been made to feel your every touch. Have I not responded as you wish?"

He cupped the sides of her breasts, lightly pulsed his hands to them, shaping them, molding them. She imagined her white flesh spilling through his long dark fingers as he pressed and caressed.

His breathing faltered the same as hers and his grip tightened though it did not hurt. "I must be certain," he said and she noted a hint of regret in his voice.

"Lest you be the next accused."

He released her breasts and pulled on the clamps, stretching her nipples. She made to apologize for speaking so boldly, but could not as a cry of surprise escaped her. The clamps seemed to dig in, to hold on. She held her breath, certain he meant to rip them off. Instead he let go and her nipples throbbed, tingled, as if tiny needles pricked them.

"Put out your hands," he said. "Feel this."

A cold, stone cylinder with a bulbous end was pressed into her hands. It was two palms long and too wide for her grip. She held it firmly, surprised by its heft, unsure what it might be.

"It will fill you."

She gasped. It could not. She shook her head fiercely as he ripped the thick rod from her hold and nudged her feet further apart.

She felt a breeze of movement as he stepped away from her, and for an instant she thought he had changed his mind. Then his hand was between her legs, slathering her with oil, his fingers probing her, coating her inside as well.

It was not a touch meant to arouse yet it did. All of his touches did. He had awakened her so thoroughly. But he did not know, he still had doubt, still feared she was marked and had marked him. She drew a long slow breath. Tried to calm her mind. Her racing heart.

She could not prove herself to him any more than she had. She could only try to show that he was not marked. That he could feel, could be as aroused as she. Mayhap she could save herself by saving him.

She raised her chin, clasped her hands tighter behind her, ready, eager to tell him what she felt, though, this time, he had yet to ask.

"I feel the oil," she said, between halting breaths, "and the heat of your hand. It is not gentle."

And then his hand was gone and she felt the pressure of the heavy rod, imagined its size as it sought entry. Her legs trembled beneath her and she held her breath, remembered the initial pain when he first entered her, was certain this would be far greater.

"You may use the table. For support."

She did so as the words left his mouth, reaching back and taking hold of the edge, the move making her more aware of the spar already inside of her as the pressure of the rod increased against her oiled passage.

"I feel afraid." She shook her head as the words spilled from her. He would know of her fear. He meant to frighten her. She knew. And he meant to test all of her senses. But all were awakened now and vying for her attention. Fear, arousal, pain, pleasure. Her chest hurt as each heaving breath forced its way into and out of her.

"You will describe it."

"It does not yield. It stretches me." The bulging end made entry with a sudden pop and her breath caught as her body adjusted, accepting it inside. "It is cold… but warming."

It entered her further and she feared her legs would fold beneath her. She widened her stance, leaned back slightly to rest more firmly against the table as he probed her further. Her head tipped back as if on its own and she breathed through her mouth, gulping in air, fearful, excited, unsure how much of its length he would demand she take.

He touched her, his fingers soft, gentle on her nether lips.

"I feel your touch..." The rod filled her slowly, steadily. "...your fingers are hot. They are spreading me." Her nipples no longer tingled. They felt numb, as if they were no longer there. The spar in her rump, wide and stout, seemed to swell as her body clenched around it. Her womb was filled, her nether lips betraying her as he removed his fingers from them and they eagerly closed around the fat rod, holding it within even as she felt him let go of it.

"What do you feel?" His voice was forced, his breath moist and hot against her face, his doublet brushing her breast, his breeches teasing her hip, igniting her where they scraped. Heat coiled within her. Her body throbbed, craved.

"I feel..." Aroused. But she dare not admit it. "...used."

His arm brushed her belly as he reached down and pulled the rod from her. And then he pushed it back in and she cried out, a weak and needy sound that revealed her surprise, her pleasure.

Her legs would not remain still. They shook. Her whole body shook.

He pulled it out of her again, then pushed it in further and she widened her stance yet more, certain he meant for her to accept it all, eager to feel it deep inside of her.

He drew it back again, slowly until it nearly pulled out of her. The bulge at the tip all but escaped her body before he filled her again. He moved it slowly, so slowly her pleasure began to hurt. It stretched her, made her nub crave to be touched. She tried to tell him, to find the right words as pain and fear became a distant thought and only need filled her mind, her body.

And then he withdrew it completely, and her nether lips throbbed as if they searched for more.

"What do you feel?" His voice was softer this time. Closer, as if his lips were near her ear.

"Empty. And…" She shook her head slowly, tried to sift through the feelings within her.

Her flesh responded to every wisp of air against it. The clamps still weighed her breasts but they no longer hurt. The stout invasion from behind made her belly feel full, her rump feel huge, stretched and yet, somehow satisfied. She tightened her muscles and felt it more. It was thick, warm, slick from the oil, and she wondered how it might feel if he moved it like he moved the huge rod in her wet passage. Sliding it out of her then back in.

"I feel…" It was wrong. These touches, these things he did to her, were to make her feel, to make himself feel. They were sinful, exquisite. Consuming. Tears of shame slid beneath the blind as she admitted the truth. "…aroused."

His fingers were gentle against her cheek as he brushed her tears away. "Do you not wish to feel aroused?"

She started to nod then shook her head, wishing her body had not betrayed her so, yet wanting as much to have its desires satisfied. "Not this way… it is wrong."

"It is wrong if you do not feel." His fingertips brushed her jaw, her neck. "These touches are meant to arouse, Abigail."

Her name came from his lips in a whisper. It lingered in the air then settled over her as the warm breath it rode on teased her neck, tormented her with a promise she hoped he would keep.

His hot palm flattened between her breasts, smoothed lower, teased her belly. "They are meant to awaken you." He cupped her core. "You must feel it, describe it." His fingers burrowed into her, reigniting her need. "If you do not, I will think you are marked. Are you marked, Abigail?"

She started to shake her head as his fingers pulsed inside of her, distracting her from everything but the sensations curling within. "These touches…"

Her muscled tightened around his fingers as they moved inside of her, making the stout spar feel even larger, and she could no longer deny how it affected her. "This thing inside of me…" She wanted it out of her, wanted him to move it within. "It makes me ache for…" She could not say. Would not.

"For what do you ache?" His words brushed her ear, warm and moist. "Tell me." He eased his fingers from her and she inched her hips forward, wanting them inside of her again. He turned her to face the table and a mere brush of his hand against her back sent her eagerly down over it, no longer caring about the clamps digging into her as she flattened against the wood. Only thinking of how his touch could satisfy the mounting lust.

His hot hand smoothed over her rump, his fingertips grazed her hip, her thigh, kneading her flesh. And then he removed the spar with one swift tug. She yelped in surprise as it popped out of her, yet she could almost still feel it inside. Then she felt the oil drip over her and he inched it inside once again. Slowly. Bit by bit. She felt every spec of it sliding forward, without pain, only fullness, an almost liquid heat pulsing through her. Then all movement stopped and she held her breath, unsure of his intention until it slid out then back inside in one steady roll of motion.

Through the haze of arousal and wonder, she heard a moan, low and desperate. He pulled it from her again, then eased it back in, and the moan came once more. It was like that of the woman in the woods. Aching and needy. Pleading...

ᴥ

The sound of her moans nearly pushed him beyond control. A witch could not feel such pleasure as this, she could not feel pleasure at all. And though her sighs and yearnings aroused him to the point of pain, he needed to feel more. To be certain of his own purity.

He pulled the stout phallus out to the bulging midpoint then slowly eased it back inside of her, nearly lying over her as he did, feeling her hot heaving breaths on his face, now close enough for him to kiss if he so chose.

He whispered to her instead. "I want to know how it feels, Abigail. Tell me clear so I will hear the truth."

"I have no words…" Her voice was breathy and pleading. The voice of defeat and desire combined. "It feels… wrong…" Her words caught as if she choked on tears. "It is sinful."

When he had first looked into her wide and frightened eyes, he saw her as an innocent. Her responses, so pure and uninhibited, should have proved that to him, but they confused him instead. And yet, it was clear, her need was nearly as great as his.

He eased the phallus out a small fraction, and she sighed. He wanted to watch as passion darkened her eyes, but knew it would be too challenging to his own control.

"If this did not bring you pleasure..." he pushed it back into her until the wide base of it stopped him. And then he pressed the heel of his hand to it, forcing the tip of it in as far as it could go, relishing the sound of her moan, and the way she flexed and rolled her hips. "...it would not bode well for you." Or for himself.

He pulled it out of her, felt her body shudder in unfulfilled need, then dropped it to the floor. He stood, smoothed his hands over her arms, urging her clasped hands apart, then lifted her to standing and wrapped his arms around her belly, holding her hot languid body against his.

From the moment he brought her into this room, he meant only to awaken her, to elicit responses that proved her innocence. He hoped to bring her pleasure, not pain. Though at times, pain was unavoidable.

"Abigail."

She breathed a reply.

"My intent is not to hurt you..." He took hold of the irons clamped to her nipples. "But this pain will grow before it will cease."

She stirred and lifted her face in his direction, as if to speak.

He did not wait for her words. "I will help you," he said, then released the clamps and threw them to the floor, aware that only a mere second would pass before sensation surged back into her breasts, filling her with unspeakable pain.

She tensed and he held her tight. And then a scream ripped through her and he turned her in his arms, leaned her back against the table, and closed his mouth over one nipple, caressing it with his tongue as she cried, soothing her as well as he could.

He cupped her other breast with his hand, squeezed it, worked his fingers over it, trying to subdue the flood of pain he knew she felt there as her hands clutched at him.

He kissed his way from one breast to the other, laved his tongue over both, then eased back, making room as she cupped them in her own hands.

"Are you well?" he asked, unable to remove his gaze from her fingers as they stroked her nipples, pinched them. Her back was arched, her chin tipped toward the ceiling. Still her fingers caressed, and he could not look away. He smoothed his hands down her length, over her hips and to her thighs. "It had to be."

"I thought I might die."

"I would have saved you."

"Can you save me still?"

He parted her legs, eased forward between them. "What would you have me do?"

"I ache…"

He cupped his hand to her core. "To be aroused so…," he said as her juices coated his fingers, "…is to admit awareness a witch could not have." He opened his breeches, rubbed her juices over the head of his cock. Would enter her slowly this time, not as he had before. And her body would respond as it did with the phallus, opening to accommodate him, sealing around him, pulling him in deeper

There would be no pain, only pleasure. For her and for him. And he would feel it all, he had to, to save his soul.

He clasped her thighs in his hands, held them wide and entered her, slowly, watching his bulging head disappear inside her wet heat.

He arched his hips, easing in further, forcing himself to move slowly, to feel every shift of her body, every tremor, every twitch of her muscles as they tightened around him, gripped him, strained against him.

And then she moaned and her body pulsed. He barely held on to control.

"You must not let go of these sensations," he said, "until you feel the heat of my seed in your womb." He eased further into her, unsure how much more he could take, these slow movements as cruel as they were exhilarating.

And then he felt her body open to him fully, welcoming him inside and his thrusts became harder, faster. Until she clenched around him and he could take no more. He jerked forward, plunging into her until he felt they might never decouple.

There was no scream from her this time, only a plea. "I cannot wait…"

"Grip me…" he said and the instant she did, wave after wave of greedy need escaped him, pulsing through his body from his head, his chest, his cock, until he felt drained of breath, of blood and seed.

"I feel it…" She writhed beneath him when he would have collapsed on top of her. "I feel your seed, hot inside of me… please…" Her head rocked side to side. "…please…"

He held firm against her, filling her until he could go no further, and when she was completely impaled, he touched her hot straining nub with his fingertips. He smoothed steady wet circles over it until her entire body stiffened and she seemed not to breathe.

"Now," he said as he grasped the tense nub and squeezed, finally granting her the pleasure he had before denied. Her body convulsed around him, pumping rhythmically, nearly bringing him to the peak again as it went on and on.

Her back arched, her small yelps of surprise grew then fell silent. The pulsing ebbed and her body fell limp. Her breasts heaved with every shuddering breath that gushed from deep inside of her.

"Good Sir…" Her voice was weak, breathy.

Still buried in her wet warmth, he leaned over her, his forearm against the table, his fingers tangled in her hair. Slowly, he drew the cloth from her eyes.

She blinked up at him before her eyes widened, seeming to search his as if in awe. "I felt everything."

As had he. She was not marked and had not marked him.

He cupped a palm to her soft cheek. Nodded slowly, finally free to make his declaration. "You are untouched by the beast."

Tears fell from her eyes as a hesitant smile curved her lips. "You have saved me."

He wiped her tears with the back of his hand then brushed her lips with his in the softest of kisses. "Mayhap," he said, "we have saved each other."

The cool damp cloth he pressed to her core as he gently washed his seed from her body soothed but did not stir. His hands, which had just tested and brought pleasure, now touched her with detached efficiency as she laid spread before him.

He had said not a word after declaring them saved. Had not looked at her after giving her another tender kiss. He had merely withdrawn from her, left her cold and wanting, then secured himself in his breeches and started to wash her.

She ached to see his eyes looking into hers once more, but feared they would be as void of heat and desire as his hands now were. Their tender time together was fleeting, and while her heart leapt at the notion of leaving this ominous space, the notion of leaving him filled her with a new kind of ache. Not in her core, but deep in her heart.

He tossed the cloth to the floor, then, without a glance her way, took her foot in his hand and slid her slipper into place. She sat up slowly as her legs dangled from the table. She watched his every move, noted the hard line of his brow, the thinning of his lips, as if heavy thoughts occupied his mind. Could their parting have created the same ache within him as in her?

His touch, warm this entire hour, was now cool as he held her other foot and slid that slipper on as well. He held it for a moment, one hand on her foot, one on her ankle, his head bowed.

"Good Sir?"

Slowly his gaze lifted to hers. She tried to understand what she saw there, in his eyes, now as cool as his touch, and worried the warm rousing feelings had been hers alone.

He stood, circled her waist with his hands and lifted her from the table. She clutched his shoulders, her gaze fixed on his. Waiting. Hoping he would speak.

He lowered her until her feet touched the floor, then opened his mouth as if to speak, but no words came from him.

With a small smile she had to force, she curtsied. Though her movement was as smooth and delicate as it could be, she knew her nakedness removed all beauty and grace from the gesture. "Thank you, Good Sir, for your diligence this hour."

He gave her a slight, silent bow in response.

"Without it," she said, "the verdict may well have been, 'guilty'."

He touched a finger to her cheek then. Drew it slowly down to her jaw. "I nearly declared it so more than once." He curled his finger below her chin, raised it slightly. "I have that regret."

She lifted herself to her toes, wanting so much to feel his arms circle her. To feel his warm breath on her cheek, his heartbeat against her breast. And then it came, his embrace. Hesitant at first, then demanding, as if he had lost some battle from within.

She held onto him, sure when she let go, he would be gone forever. "What will happen to me now?" she asked, unsure what she sought in response.

"They will no longer shun you," he said. "Though you will not speak of this hour past."

She shook her head against his shoulder. Whispered her reply. "I will not."

He loosened his hold on her, eased back, leaving her no choice but to withdraw from his warmth.

"They wait," he said, then slowly dipped his head to hers.

She stretched to meet him, eager to receive his offered kiss. His lips were firm but soft, as they had been before, only this time he did not break away so soon. His mouth moved on hers, gently, molding her lips, blending their breaths, until every sigh, every heartbeat, every touch made them as one. She would have willingly remained there, no longer an accused with her examiner, but a woman in the arms of the man she had dreamed of, whose touch filled her with pleasures she could not have imagined. Who responded to her touches the same.

He deepened the kiss, his tongue caressing hers the same as his hands caressed her back, softly, firmly, longingly. And then he pulled away.

She wanted more, greedy in her desire. Wished that when this night was through he would find her again. Take her. Keep her.

His gaze still on hers, he offered his arm. She hesitated before accepting it, unsure how far he would escort her while she wore nothing more than soft slippers and a flush of passion. Her step faltered as they reached the chamber door.

She withdrew her arm from his and stood back, certain he did not mean to bring her outside unclothed.

"You will be dressed," he said as if hearing her thoughts.

He opened the door and, with a hand at her back, led her into the main hall.

She looked at the settee beside the wide stair, hoped to see a shift, bodice or petticoats draped over it. She looked ahead for a full wardrobe, a cloak on a peg, something to shield her. There was nothing. Only a cold empty hall.

She turned to him, knew the question was clear in her eyes.

His gaze was on hers, tender now and thoughtful, though not nearly as warm as she wished. A small smile tugged at his lips. It was not a happy look. And then he lifted his hands slowly and cupped her breasts. She sighed and he kneaded them gently, then drew his fingertips over the marks still evident there.

"You must be brave," he said, then dropped his hands from her. "Before you are clothed, they will see how well you have been tested."

Was there no end to this shaming? She started to speak, to ask why, if he would proclaim her innocent, she should have to endure such humiliation. But his hand, gripping hers and gently squeezing, silenced her words, her pleas, telling her there would be no other way.

She closed her eyes, tried to find some hidden strength. She had endured much at his hands. Her body and mind both tested. She could endure this. She would have no choice. "They will but look?"

"They will dress you."

She lifted her gaze to his, and the discomfort she saw in his eyes was comfort to her heart, for it was proof he felt at least some regret for her unease.

She drew a long slow breath, trying to find her courage. Standing tall, she raised her chin. Resigned to face these final moments with humble poise.

He curled her fingers into the crook of his elbow. "It is time," he said, then opened the front doors.

The pungent odor of dankness and pitch wafted in from the gated yard. The crowd, mocking the women still bound and spread with their breasts bared, seemed not to notice how she stood naked beside their regal governor.

The cold wet air clung to her skin, made her shiver and ache for the warmth of her governor's embrace.

Then soft whimpers from one of the accused reached her like a hopeless plea, and she ached to assure her the hardest part of this examination would be the shame. Unless her body had been marked.

She gave a quick glance at Jameson, her governor, her examiner, and wondered if he would be as patient and diligent with the others as he had been with her. Would he kiss them as well? Take them with the same passionate fervor? She clenched her eyes, not wanting to know. Not wanting to think it was the same for him with all the accused but that she had been someone for whom he truly cared.

Her body shuddered in fear, cold and regret, and he shifted, took her hand from his arm and led her to the edge of the top stair. He stood unmoving, then drew a breath that swelled his chest and called out to the rowdy crowd. "Who will clothe this innocent woman?"

The crowd grew silent and she grew weak as all eyes turned in her direction, touching her in a near tangible way, heating her flesh despite the cold, making her shiver and crave cover. And then Jameson took her hand and led her down the stairs as the crowd broke into a deafening cheer.

Four women came forward with clothes, the midwife, her daughter and others. Jameson urged three to properly clothe her, and sent the other to prepare the room for the next examination.

Hands were on her everywhere, cold hands, hot hands, rough and probing. They touched the welts on her breasts, pinched her still-tender nipples, brushed her sore rump and probed her shaven core. Murmurs of appreciation surrounded her the whole time. She kept her chin high, did not look into their eyes, did not close her own. They would see how well she had been tested, he warned her, promised her, and once they were through, they would dress her and she would no longer be shunned.

She shifted a glance his way and saw him watching as she was touched, examined further by these noisy, gruff women. And then she was pulled this way and that as layers of clothes were draped over her. A new shift, and petticoats. A bodice without stays. They dressed her most properly, yet left her head uncovered, her slippered feet so adorned. And then they moved as one toward the governor, taking her with them, leaving her there, before they rejoined the crowd.

His gaze locked on hers as he offered his arm then led her toward the gate. How would she stand amongst the very people who had touched her breasts and mocked her when he had paraded her before them? She could not bear it, did not want to be one of those people cheering as the others were bared. She hesitated as they drew closer to the gate.

"There is not time," he said for her ears only, then looked toward the sky. "There are but few hours before the sun will rise." Unease deepened his voice. "And five accused still wait."

He took her beyond the gate and made to withdraw his arm. She did not let go and he faced her, his eyes hard, impatient.

"Good Sir," she said with a slight bow of her head, "if it pleases you, I offer my help."

He gaze went wide, his lips thin. And then he drew himself taller, lowering his eyes to still see her. "It is for myself alone to determine innocence or guilt."

She shook her head. Ignored the murmur rumbling through the crowd.

"I would not dare make a proclamation," she said. "I would merely assist, for have I not learned a great deal through your examination of me?"

Without a hint as to his thoughts, he turned away, his steady determined stride taking him to the next woman in line. "Cut her loose!" he shouted to the watchman who quickly obeyed. "Have these good people inspected the accused?"

The watchman, frightening in his black hood, leather-clad chest and bare bulging arms, untied the tearful Rebecca Lilly. "They have," he said.

Abigail could only watch in pained silence as the frightened young woman was handed to her governor. Timid and chaste, Rebecca would crumble at the very sight of the crop, if not at his command to disrobe.

The image of that shot painful daggers of jealousy through Abigail's heart. And though only pity should have filled her, she felt trembling grief, wishing not to know he would do the same to the others as he had done to her. Yet even as tears threatened, she watched him touch Rebecca's breasts, seeming unmoved by the girl's stream of tears. And then he stood behind her and pulled her dress down to the elbows, and Abigail recalled the horror of being bared so boldly.

He steered Rebecca toward the crowd, his eyes on Abigail's as he stopped directly in front of her. She did not look away, could not, wanted to know his thoughts and waited for him to speak them.

He simply stared down at her as if choosing his words carefully. "We begin here," he said, finally. "Then you will follow us inside." He gave Rebecca a nudge that forced her closer to Abigail. "Be this a witch?"

Abigail looked into Rebecca's frightened eyes, then lowered her gaze to the girl's ripe breasts, thrust out before her.

His exasperated sigh drew her attention. "Time does not wait," he said.

At his words, she raised her hands and closed her fingers over Rebecca's nipples. She pinched hard, then smiled in relief at the girl's shocked gasp. She glanced at Jameson, saw the look of approval in his eyes, then turned back to Rebecca.

"Do not fear," Abigail said softly. "The governor and I will take great care to prove your innocence this hour."

About the Author

Arla Dahl is a lover and avid reader of all things sexy and suspenseful. In her Immoral Virtue Trilogy, the horrors of the 17th Century witch trials are exposed, examined and reversed. Deeply moved by the viciousness of times, Arla created stories that would turn history on its ear and make that which labeled the accused susceptible to the temptations of evil, into the one thing that would set them free. Lust.

Stay engaged!

Find Arla online

Facebook at www.facebook.com/arladahl

Twitter: https://twitter.com/ArlaDahlAuthor

Her blog: http://www.arladahl.com/notes/

See also, her website

www.arladahl.com

Arla **Dahl**

Immoral Virtue Series
Book Two

The Accused

"Wherefore for the sake of fulfilling their lusts
(women) consort even with devils."
-Heinrich Kramer, 1486 "Malleus Maleficarum"
(The Hammer of Witches)

EXCERPT
The Accused (Immoral Virtue, #2)

"Enough!" With mercy, they reached the end of the line and the watchman pulled Elizabeth beyond the crowd's longest stretch. "Who would deny her breasts are pure?" When no one spoke, he tugged her backward.

She gratefully let him take her to where the air was cooler, the roar of the crowd less deafening. Relieved to have passed the first examination.

She did not struggle as he bound her wrists to the X once more. Nor did she resist when he spread her legs wide and secured her ankles, nor when he tucked her shift in at her sides, assuring a clear view for the crowd of her now sore and sullied flesh.

Perhaps, the worst had passed. She closed her eyes for a brief moment, comforting herself with the thought that, somehow, the rest of her examination would be better, inside, with the governor.

There was movement from the manor. A hush fell around her as all eyes turned toward it.

Governor Jameson Foster stood tall and proud atop the stairs, regal in his quilted doublet and fitted breeches, while a naked Abigail Prescott stood brave and poised beside him. Her breasts bore the marks of severe testing. Her body glistened as though coated with oils. Her pubis was bald as though all the hair had been stripped from her. The sight filled Elizabeth with dread for she feared the worst might still be yet to come.

Governor Foster led Abigail down the stairs, his dark eyes slowly skimming the crowd before resting on the women with Elizabeth, bound, bared and afraid. He turned back to the crowd with Abigail beside him, and called out, "Who will clothe this innocent woman?"

Shouts and cheers rang out as several women rushed forward to dress Abigail. Elizabeth shared tearful smiles with those bound beside her, relieved to know the first among them to be examined had been found unmarked and innocent.

The watchman cut the restraints of another, the frightened Rebecca, hardly twenty, fair of complexion and hair. He passed her into the governor's charge, and the governor touched his large hands to her breasts, caressing them, weighing them. Inspecting them much as the watchman and the crowd had done before. And then he led her to the gate and Elizabeth feared he would make her walk the line yet again. Instead, he beckoned Abigail, now properly dressed and standing with the crowd. She went to him, the top of her head barely reaching his shoulder. He spoke to her, seemed to grow impatient. And then Abigail reached out and touched the girl's breasts, hesitantly at first then with an eagerness Elizabeth did not understand.

The girl trembled but did not resist as Abigail's fingers sunk into her white flesh, kneading her, caressing her, pinching her. Abigail murmured something, and the governor nodded, his dark expression softening with a near tender approval.

Elizabeth trembled with concern. While in the manor, had he stirred Abigail with touches as soft as the watchman's? Could she permit the governor to do the same to her? To see her completely bare? To touch her? Shave her? Fill her with desire she should not feel? She would resist, deny all budding sensations…

But it is only a witch who does not feel…

As if hearing her thoughts, the governor turned, looked where she stood bound, and settled his gaze upon hers. His eyes were unlike that of the watchman.

They held no tenderness. No compassion. Only suspicion, resolve and authority. She bowed her head breaking the contact, then closed her eyes, aware his unyielding gaze still lingered upon her. The strength of it heated her body in ways it should not, and though she tried to discourage all thoughts of submitting to his examination, she knew, to prove her innocence, there would be no other way.

When she dared a glance back, he had turned away, his stride wide and unhurried, as he led a bare-breasted Rebecca toward the manor. Abigail lingered a moment then followed, her skirts hoisted to her ankles as she tread quickly to the governor's side. She spoke to him as they climbed the stairs. He seemed not to respond and she spoke again, her voice fading as the trio disappeared into the manor.

Arla Dahl

Arla Dahl

www.ingramcontent.com/pod-product-compliance
Lightning Source LLC
Chambersburg PA
CBHW030539130626
46552CB00006B/2333

* 9 7 8 0 9 9 0 4 0 1 6 3 6 *